Praise for

"An extremely powerful story focusing on a young woman working towards her goals in a neurotypical world. Noori truly does have it all, the story telling provides a raw glimpse into the experience of individuals on a spectrum."

—Anam
Friend and neurospicy beta-reader

"An incredibly relatable read! *Noori has it all* is an intimate portrayal of the life of person with ADHD and I felt myself relating to her every step of the way! The author keeps it interesting, making it both informative and a comforting read for those with ADHD. Highly recommend!"

—Maariyah
Friend and fellow ADHDer

"Vibrant, heartwarming and undeniably entertaining! Amani Noor's debut novella expertly balances light-hearted fun and comforting sincerity. This author is definitely one to watch!"

—Leesa
Friend and cover designer

"Wholesome, funny, and cosy - everything I love in a slice-of-life novella. Amani expertly draws on her own experiences with ADHD and lends her voice to Noori - a beloved character, pursuing her dreams of animating 'Errant's Law', her passion project, and all the obstacles that come with trying to do so. A wonderful debut, and I cannot wait to see more from the author."

—Sid
Friend and fellow writer

Noor HAS IT ALL?!!

AMANI NOOR

ISBN-13: 9781068522413

For my neurospicy girlies and fellow perfectionists.
For those who made asking for help no longer feel like the worst thing in the world.

When stopping time, two laws that must be followed.

1. Stop time when it is absolutely necessary.
2. When you take time, you must give it back.

1 NOORI JUST WANTED A SIMPLE LIFE

She could see it now. She was sitting in a plush chair, popcorn in one hand, nachos in the other. This time she was wearing an autumnal-themed dress with ombre tulle skirts. Her friends and family would be beside her. In fact, everyone who had the fortune (or misfortune) to hear Noori talk about her life's work would be invited. Together, they would watch *Errant's Law*, the animation she had been working on, unfold on the big screen, making her childhood dreams come true.

Noori could see it all in her mind's eye and what a beautiful sight it was.

She didn't know if she would be so enraptured by her tale unfolding in front of her that she would forget to eat or if she would eat everything because she was excited and overwhelmed. She didn't know if she preferred having almost everyone she knew sit beside her as she watched or if she preferred to be on her lonesome. She did know that she would have to pack tissues. It wasn't a sad story, but it was hers. She would weep because it was hers.

She always wanted to do something huge, leave a mark on the world, to show herself off, to them, and to herself. She knew she was still ways away yet, but she couldn't help it. She was closer than she had ever been before, and her mind couldn't resist the urge to run wild and free in awe of it.

Noori imagined herself at the afterparty, where she didn't know if she would sob the whole time or be so overwhelmed with emotion that she would dissociate. She knew, at least, that she would dance and scream and shout and pray no one was taking a video. It would all be a dream come true.

She sighed in bliss, warmth filling her and making her giddy. Noori couldn't wait to continue her journey to get where she needed to go. She couldn't wait. She *couldn't* wait. She'd submitted a snippet of the animation to an annual expo where there would be a showcase for promising animators, and she had passed the preliminary screening and thus gotten an invite to attend with her project. While the seed for *Errant's Law* had been planted while she was an undergraduate student, she had been to the expo with a cousin in her younger years. She had enjoyed drawing as a child but found drawing still images boring. The expo had showed her something that she, an everyday person, could do with her interest and now she would go back as an artist.

All she had to do was make it perfect and submit it to them before the next deadline. The rest was history.

Noori's phone buzzed in her hand, dissolving her thoughts and pulling her back to reality. She peered around, realising that she was standing in the middle of her apartment, probably with a destination in mind before she'd stopped and submerged into what she hoped would be her upcoming future.

Had she taken her ADHD medication today?

Noori pressed her lips together. The reasons behind her standing here could be endless. She walked towards her small kitchen and looked around. Her gaze caught on the checklist on her fridge, and she realised in fact that she hadn't taken her meds and that was probably what she had been planning to do.

She pulled one of the meals she had prepped out of her fridge and heated it up. While she waited, she remembered her phone had buzzed so she checked her messages. She had one from her friend Emaya.

Hey Noori, random question but I thought you'd have the answer

What's the best place for pottery painting?

Noori smiled as she sent a response and then another and another. Telling her friend also about the experiences of the places she had gone, their opening hours and if there was anything else around the area that was interesting.

Emaya sent a laughing emoji. *See! I knew you'd know. Thanks*

Pleased, Noori settled to eat, but a knock on the door stopped her from burning her tongue from her impatience at the steaming food.

She frowned. She wasn't anticipating any visitors, unless it was one of her neighbours. She looked down at her state of dress, her favourite frog pyjamas, and couldn't see any stains. Surely at this hour, it was socially acceptable enough?

She tiptoed to the door as the person knocked again. Holding her breath, she spied through the peephole and saw someone dressed in black, a silver crest embroidered on their chest, signifying that they were an agent from the Universal Time Alliance.

Noori stilled.

A visit from them wasn't good. She could pretend she wasn't home. That way they couldn't hurt her. Not that she imagined they would beat her up unprovoked, but she suspected they weren't here to be nice.

As quietly as she could, she moved back to the table to eat her food. Her eyes shifted to the door every couple of seconds as if the agent would just barge through.

The Universal Time Alliance would only be here if there was a serious problem with her time usage. Noori didn't have such a problem, so they were probably at the wrong door. She decided that she would sit it out and wait for them to leave.

Minutes passed and they continued to knock every ten seconds or so like clockwork. She couldn't imagine why they were here. She had done no wrong.

Was she a witness to a crime?

No.

Well, even if she was, why would the Universal Time Alliance be here?

She bit her lip and poured herself some juice. They knocked again and Noori's head whipped to the door as if it was a surprise. The movement caused the juice to splash on her hand and sleeve, making her grumble, the wet sensation making her skin crawl and senses heighten.

She snatched a towel off the counter top and dried her hand thoroughly before gulping down her medication with whatever juice was in the cup. Afterwards, she ticked her medication chart.

They knocked on the door again.

She suspected they weren't going to leave, and she didn't want them to ruin her jam by periodically knocking on her door. She had plans, she was a busy woman! She was going to work on *Errant's Law*, tidy her whole flat, go to the gym, clean her car, watch TV, make more meals for the week and do her laundry. She didn't have time for this.

Maybe she should call the police? Say she was being harassed? But would the claims be baseless because it wasn't like she had spoken to the agent?

They knocked again and Noori wanted to cry.

This slow-burn tactic of torture was both angering and upsetting her, and while answering the door was a possible quick solution, she was worried that maybe it was not, and that she would then have a problem on her hands.

Though, really, she kind of already had a problem on her hands, didn't she?

In a rush of determination which Noori was all too happy to exploit, she rapidly combed her fingers through her unruly dark hair and marched towards the door. She ensured the chain was on and then gently opened it an inch, all while sporting a sharp gaze which probably looked more like she was confused.

"Sorry, can I help you?" she enquired, trying to sound firm and assertive but to her own ears she just sounded rude, and it made guilt claw at her.

"May I speak to Ms Noori Ilyas?" the man said, betraying no emotion in his voice or even on his face.

Noori's fingers on the latch were shaking.

"Depends—I mean, I can pass on a message." Noori hoped they didn't catch her slip.

The man who looked to be a very similar age to Noori now appeared tired, probably due to having to knock on multiple people's doors to convey messages and being greeted by people like her. Noori wondered if he was paid enough for it.

He opened a file that Noori hadn't noticed he was holding and looked down at a page, then at Noori, the page again and then at Noori.

Noori realised he was probably looking at a picture of her.

Shit, this is so embarrassing.

"Ms Noori Ilyas," he stated, now sounding tired and giving her an unimpressed look.

Noori shuffled on her feet, wanting to die.

"Mr Universal Time Alliance person thing—I mean, person," she greeted, hoping to hold the same level of coolness in her composure as he did.

How does he do it? Is it the uniform? Does he take classes? Can I take classes—

"You have accrued a significant time debt and have not answered the summons that we have sent numerous times by post."

"Huh?" A chill ran through Noori as her mind raced.

Noori had covered up the timer on her wrist with a tight wristband a long time ago and because of it, often neglected to check it, and in the few moments she did, it just made her anxious. So anxious she would pause time to calm down from the all-consuming dread and shame.

Everyone could pause time, but it was restrictive when you did. You couldn't move anything unless you already had it in your hand and it was small. The internet froze too. You also couldn't really change anything about the world around you. However, in the rare occurrence that you did try to change the world, you would have immediate consequences after you resumed time. But it was handy when you needed to fill in forms or complete homework.

Most importantly, when you paused time, every second was counted and recorded on your wrist, and this was monitored by the Universal Time Alliance—the international organisation that oversaw everyone's usage.

Noori's heart was thumping and she was starting to sweat.

It was then Noori remembered that she couldn't remember the last time she had collected her letters from her mailbox below, and frankly, she had forgotten about it until this moment. The parcels she ordered never fit inside, and she believed that in the year 2024 no person truly had the reason to contact her via mail when email existed.

Second of all, was he really saying all of this on her doorstep? He might as well tell everyone her business! She had a mind to let him in but at the same time, she severely didn't want to. Even if he was just the messenger, he didn't deserve such comforts.

"Excuse me?"

"You have accrued a time debt of—"

"Stop yes, I can check that myself," Noori snapped, her voice low and hopeful that no one could overhear. She felt her wrist burn as if it was reminding her that she had such a debt.

Though could she really say she was surprised? She really did pause time as if she had all the time in the world.

"Sorry, I just..." Noori started, feeling bad that she'd snapped. It wasn't his fault, even if she wanted to blame him. "I'm processing."

She needed more than a minute. She needed to pause time and to never play it again.

"Is that all you're here to tell me?" she asked, feeling sick and wanting to lie down. She had a mind to close the door and terminate the chance of the conversation getting any worse.

"You are summoned to court where you will face sanctions for your usage," he answered simply, easily, as if he wasn't handing her a death sentence. He took a thick envelope out of the file and passed it to her. "The details of the court case will be in the letter enclosed. Inside there will also be a booklet which will have other useful information that we advise you go over."

Noori stared at the envelope. Surely if she didn't take it off him, the whole thing didn't exist, right?

The man appeared to read the rationale behind her hesitation. "Please take the envelope."

Noori cringed. *But I don't want to!*

"Even so, you could get into more trouble if you resist. I would also just slip it under your door."

Noori looked up at him. Had she said that aloud?

She sighed, took the envelope and then shut the door in the man's face, giving him only a brief goodbye as she did, hoping he didn't get offended. Then, in her apartment by herself, she dashed the envelope away as if it was a hot potato, and she sank to the ground, her face buried in her hands as she considered the predicament she had gotten herself into.

~ ⌛ ~

The situation festered in Noori's mind before she did anything about it. She had blocked the day to get things done, with the main focus being *Errant's Law*. However, as she sat at her workstation, poised and ready, her mind went to the envelope that was lying somewhere on the floor in her kitchen. She told herself that it was okay and 'it is what it is' but Noori didn't know what it was, and she wasn't prepared to find out. She also knew nothing was going to change with it lying on the floor. It appeared she would have to face it at some point.

After an unproductive couple of hours, she opened the envelope and read the contents. The court date was the same time as the deadline for her project, so now she had two things she needed to prepare for. *Amazing*. She read the letter multiple times, the bold and stern font making Noori quiver under her blanket.

While she understood the outcome to be quite rare, once she peeked at the number on her wrist, she knew she was going to jail, and her life was over.

She glanced at the booklet that they had enclosed, which appeared to be something that could be helpful. However, before reading it properly, she had left it on the arm of the couch, meaning that it had inevitably gotten knocked down. Now it was in between the couch and the wall and while it was an easy rescue mission to retrieve it, Noori wasn't in the mood to be heroic.

Not knowing what else to do apart from making an appointment to talk about it with an advisor, she texted her friends, and it wasn't long before she found herself on the couch at her friend Kiran's house, unloading the matter in the way she always disclosed things. Telling them it wasn't serious at all, whilst overplaying her reaction.

"Death is coming for me," Noori declared. She buried her face in her hands, lamenting her fate. Her lowered gaze caught onto an ambiguous dried paint pattern on the carpet by her feet and her mind latched on the mystery of unravelling what it could be.

"You are not going to die," Kiran said, her tone wholly unconcerned as she poured her homemade chai into mugs for herself and her three visitors.

"They're going to kill me," she insisted, still entranced by the pattern. *It kind of looks like a cat lying down?*

"They're not going to kill you. Arrest you? Maybe. Trial and prosecute you? Most likely. Throw you behind bars? I can totally see that happening," her other friend, Layla, who sat beside her on the couch, said. In her lap was a fluffy pillow which she was combing through with one hand. Her phone was in the other.

Noori looked up and frowned at Kiran and Layla who laughed, but she couldn't stop a little giggle from escaping her too.

Kiran gave out the mugs and sat in her weathered armchair, the seat she never shared with anyone.

"Prison orange is not my colour," Noori persisted, wrapping her hands around the mug. She hummed to herself. It was such a beautiful temperature.

"It's totally your colour," Emaya disagreed, a smile clear in her voice. Noori rolled her eyes, but also felt the absence of something in her mind. What was she thinking about again? Aside from the impending matter of her potential incarceration? She looked around as if to find something that had had her attention just moments before. Her gaze skimmed past the flecks of paint in the carpet, but no recollection came to mind.

She frowned, but then shrugged and let it go. Maybe she would remember later.

"Girls, I'm being serious! I thought I was going to die. It was so—" Noori shuddered as she remembered the encounter. All in all, as she reflected on the matter, the man seemed like an all-around alright person, but the situation was so unnerving. Did they *really* come to her home and deliver the message? What was she, royalty? Why didn't they call her? Why didn't they just send an email? She was good at those. "Weird," she finished. "I can't believe they came to my home. Don't they have better things to do?"

"Well, you didn't check your mail, and they wanted to make sure you knew. Imagine you missed the court hearing?" Emaya mused, taking a sip of her drink.

Noori pressed her lips together. That would be horrifying. She really needed to check her mail as soon as she got home.

"I feel like they are being dramatic anyway." Noori shrugged as she spoke. "I only have a bit of time debt."

"A bit?" Kiran questioned. Noori didn't have to turn to see she was arching her eyebrows. "Hun, they would not be personally visiting you if you only had a bit."

"Yeah," Layla agreed and she looked up from her phone. She had stated that she was searching for something online a couple of minutes prior, probably to do with the situation. Noori couldn't quite remember what that was, and she wondered if her friend even knew what she was doing on her phone either. Sometimes, they really did have the same brain. "You didn't tell us how much you accrued."

Noori bit her lip. Her fists were curled, and her body was tense. She felt sick and full of regret. Her eyes burned and she had the all-consuming urge to be living a life—someone else's life—instead of her own at that moment.

She pushed the feeling away. She was becoming dysregulated and reactive—she trusted her friends with everything, but that was usually when she had dissociated from the matter. Maybe she shouldn't have brought it up at all. Maybe she should just go home and potentially never speak to her friends ever again.

"It was only a couple of um—nothing to worry—"

"Noori," said Kiran's warning voice.

"It was two."

"Months?" Emaya guessed.

"Years..."

"What?" all three girls responded at once. Noori's face warmed, her armpits sweated (had she put deodorant on today?) and her whole body vibrated from stress.

"I mean, yeah."

God, this was awful, awful, awful. Noori looked back down and saw the painted silhouette of the lying cat. How interesting it was that Kiran had inadvertently made the mark on the carpet. Unless her friend did it on purpose? But Noori couldn't think about how it might've happened by accident. Kiran was amazing at art so there was no way that could've happened.

Unless it was a new art style, or she copied something?

But why was Kiran painting on the carpet? *I should ask.*

"What do you do when you pause time?" Layla asked, putting her phone down. Her fingers still combing through the fluffy pillow.

Noori bit her lip, trying to remember the last time she did and what she was doing. She rubbed the wristband that covered her debt, suddenly remembering exactly when she had last used—abused—time.

"I was running late on the way to work yesterday and couldn't make my mind up on what to wear," she said nonchalantly, feeling quite justified and conveniently forgetting the fact she was always late and always needed extra time to think. "Surely we all do the same."

Emaya shrugged. "I just let myself be late to things. It is what it is."

Noori admired her friend's attitude and wished she had that much chill. The four of them considered themselves neurodivergent in some way, with Noori dubbing their group chat *Neurospice Girls*. She and Emaya both had a diagnosis of ADHD and while they had had numerous discussions about how similar their brains were, they presented differently. Noori always ran with anxiety that her life was ending, and Emaya tended to burn bridges when she got there. Noori just wanted a simple life and didn't want people to hate her.

"Have you spoken to your doctor?" Kiran asked.

"Why would I do that?"

"Why not? Can't she write you a doctor's note about your diagnosis?"

Noori pondered for a second. That wasn't a bad idea. Though, she considered that maybe it would be a matter of if rather than when—that is, she wasn't sure that was something Dr Vallant would do. However, Noori remembered that actually maybe she should've declared her diagnosis to the Universal Time Alliance like she was advised, and then maybe some paperwork would be sent to her doctor to fill in, and maybe she wouldn't be in this predicament at all.

"I feel kind of bad because I'm always asking her for something."

"That's her job," Layla pointed out. "Are you still embarrassed that you dreamt that you and she were besties?"

Noori blinked and turned to her friend. Since when had she told her that? God, she really needed to learn to shut up sometimes.

"First of all, it was a very wholesome dream we spent the whole day together and had brunch and everything. Second of all, please never mention that to me ever again." Feeling red, she gave her friends a meaningful look. "All of you."

They laughed and Noori joined in. She couldn't remember the dream well, and she was grateful for it because her mind liked to remind her of it every time she had an appointment.

"Wait, have you been taking your medication?" Emaya asked.

"Of course I have!" Noori said, remembering that she had logged it this morning on her checklist. Or was that yesterday?

No, she knew it was today because she had spilt juice, and somehow, she could still smell it.

"I take it every day," Noori continued, the lie coming out of her almost too easily. "But you know, the medication makes me hyperfocus too. That's hardly my fault."

She didn't forget the time when she'd taken her medication and focused on learning calligraphy and at one point, she had paused time so she could achieve perfection. It was probably the tip of the slippery slope that had got her into this mess.

"Okay, why don't we think about a plan?" Kiran suggested.

"Yeah," Emaya said. "Why don't you speed up nights?"

"My doctor got mad at me for not sleeping." Noori remembered complaining to her doctor about the medication not being that effective anymore. That maybe she needed a higher dose. On further enquiry on her doctor's part, she had found out Noori had skipped three nights of sleep every week since the last time she had seen her. Her doctor had advised her to sleep every night until their next regular check-up before she made any changes to her medication plan, and the advice had worked wonders too. Noori had forgotten how nice it felt to be well rested and the medication she took did work better because of it.

Who knew generic advice from healthcare professionals was actually valid? She had been advising everyone around her to adhere to good sleep hygiene ever since.

"I'm sure if you sped up one night every couple of weeks, no one would notice, especially if you had a lie-in at the weekends," Layla suggested.

Noori sighed. "That would hardly reduce my debt and not only that, I am still working on my baby."

The atmosphere of the room changed as she mentioned her project. Her friends' eyes all lit up and it made Noori giddy with delight.

"How is it going?" Kiran asked.

Noori beamed, a surge of euphoria consuming her and making her want to screech. She tightened her fists to withstand the urge to make any non-human-like noises.

"Girls," she started, her voice as daydreamy as the look in her eyes. She took a sip of her chai which she realised was still too hot but its burn didn't bother her. "I'm going to be famous and rich, and I won't have to work another day in my life—out of obligation—ever again." Noori had been having the time of her life thinking about her early retirement plan. She had so many things she wanted to do that it was starting to keep her up at night, stressed. "I know I'm just being delusional, but I am having so much fun with it."

"As you should. You've been talking about it forever," Kiran said, a smile clear in her voice. "I remember the day you told me all about it after your marketing exam."

Noori smiled. She remembered that too and she was still amazed to this day that she'd passed the exam.

"And the relationship you have had with it has been completely toxic," Emaya noted, now having finished her drink and put it on the side. "But it's the only thing I wouldn't mind you getting back together with."

Noori laughed. "Also, I'm basically, nearly, pretty much finished, meaning..."

"We can watch it?" all three of them said at once, making Noori love them more. She couldn't decide who was more excited, her or them.

"Yes!" Noori declared and put down her mug. She jumped up from her seat and started pacing the room. "I'm going to organise a watch party with all four of us, and it's going to be like an actual real-life movie." She couldn't wait. She *couldn't* wait!

"I'm pretty sure it's already a real movie," Layla stated. She got up and grabbed Noori's hands and squeezed them. "It's going to be so good."

Noori almost squealed. "I know, but I'm going to dim the lights and provide snacks and everything." She squeezed Layla's hands back and then turned to Emaya and Kiran, who had also gotten up. "You all must tell me what you think, but remember I only accept positive feedback. We're too close to the deadline for anything wrong or bad."

She smiled. Just thinking about *Errant's Law* gave her so much free dopamine. It was one thing which, despite the inconsistencies over the years, she had tried her best to keep faithful to despite numerous other entanglements along the way. In the end, it had worked out and she had now completed something.

She had loved making cartoons for as long as she could remember. It was her favourite thing to do but she had never been consistent with it. When she was diagnosed with ADHD and had gotten medicated, her life changed for the better. She was able to *do* things now instead of just meandering around like a sim waiting for instruction. She could also see things through, pay attention when people were speaking to her and the crippling self-doubt which came from all the noise in her head no longer tormented her.

She was still pretty inconsistent and had a love-hate relationship with work, but things had improved so much for the better. She was managing and was now able to do things she had once dreamt of.

All in all, things *were* pretty good.

She just hoped her court hearing wouldn't get in the way of her baby, because otherwise, what was the point of anything at all?

The whole 'Time Alliance' thing was just a minor setback and something she could figure out herself. It was probably something that could be rectified easily.

"Are you sure your debt won't get in the way of it? Your court date is on the same day as the submission," Kiran asked, concerned.

"This is Noori after all," Emaya considered. "If anyone's got this, it's definitely you."

Feeling a sense of pride, Noori dramatically flicked her hair over her shoulder. "I made an appointment with one of them—one of the people, an advisor?" She smiled easily. She was just *so* organised that she had no choice but to be proud of herself. "Don't worry, girls. I got this."

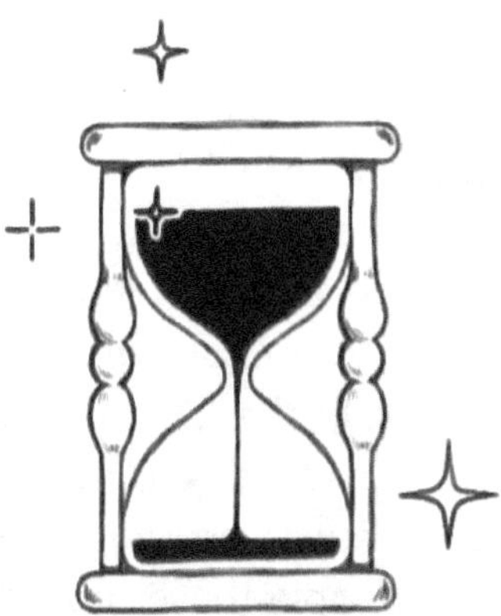

2 SHE WAS JUST LIKE EVERYONE ELSE

Noori did not "got this".

She sat affronted opposite the advisor person thing with whom she had an appointment to solve all her problems.

"Wait, wait, wait, say that again?" Noori stammered, her heart now racing and her mind whizzing with thoughts.

"Your debt will not be waived," the advisor said. He sat taller than her and age had wrinkled his face.

Noori took in a deep breath, though it did little to calm her tense shoulders and the increasing urge to shake and fidget with everything in sight. Bouncing off the walls and swinging from the light also felt like a good idea too. Instead, she started to shake her leg.

"But I have ADHD," she said, gesturing to the old diagnosis letter she had once been given. She had spent half the night looking for it only to find it safely filed away in her clearly labelled, overflowing 'important files' folder.

The man was not impressed, and she could tell from the crease in between his brows. She could also tell that he had an interesting taste in what styled hair looked like—if he did brush his hair? *Does he own a brush?*

She knew that she shouldn't judge but regardless of what he thought was acceptable, which was valid because it *was* the year 2024, she just didn't agree with it. Someone's messy hair wasn't a cancellable offence, was it? Unless it was? She was no longer updated with the ways of the young people these days. Anyway, she was desperate, undeniably, irrevocably *desperate* to brush his hair. She needed to do it more than she needed to breathe, and it just upset her that it wouldn't be socially acceptable to do such a thing. She didn't need to go to court for two offences.

"Regardless of your condition," he started. Noori frowned. She wouldn't call ADHD a condition. She considered it more of a way of life and state of being throughout the universe. "You have declared that you are of sound mind when you are pausing time. Unless you retract your statement then you would have to go through other proceedings."

Noori cringed. She imagined that saying now that she wasn't of sound mind would put her in more trouble, and then she would definitely be jailed for defamation, and she'd have to then spend the rest of her life there and she'd be stripped of her ability to pause time. She might just pass away after that. And truly, she *was* of sound mind. Though she wondered what would happen if she stated that she was not of sound mind but then they investigated it, and they found out that she was? Would it just cancel out? She would have to google it later.

"I am of sound mind yes," she said. "Are you? I mean! Surely the diagnosis counts for something, right?" She winced – what was she saying? Did she ever think before she spoke?

The man, whose name Noori could still not remember despite asking him three times, let out a sigh. "There are things you can do. Have you read over the information booklet we give to everyone with a summons letter?"

Noori cast her mind back. There was a booklet? She couldn't remember and she knew that she definitely wouldn't have read it—who had time or the mental space and emotional capacity for that? Not her.

She shook her head. "There was a letter—I mean, I got the letter, but I didn't, with the booklet. I mean, I don't know anything about the booklet. I haven't, I haven't read it." She was getting nervous, and it was only making her want to slap herself. Why was it taking her so long to say one thing? She wanted to throw herself away. This whole thing was a waste of time.

She then suddenly remembered that she did, in fact, have a booklet which was still waiting for rescue. She didn't confess this though. She was convinced the man thought her to be an idiot. She didn't want him to think she was a liar too.

The man let out a loud breath, making Noori twitch in her seat. She shifted her position and then again, suddenly uncomfortable.

"Time debts are serious offences which can lead to severe consequences, including prison time. I would advise you to have a serious think about your course of action and to properly prepare yourself for the hearing."

Noori felt as small as a child, tiny in a chair opposite her headteacher who was telling her off for wandering around during lessons and distracting her classmates.

She played with her fingers and her legs were shaking. She shifted in her seat again and she couldn't get the thick soreness out of her throat enough to speak. She nodded in response and used her short, unruly hair as a curtain.

Noori blinked, feeling full of raw emotion, and found that there was now a booklet in front of her. She must have blanked out—something that still happened periodically when she was medicated. She would reflect on what her attention span was like before but she couldn't remember.

She put her emotions in a box and shoved it away in her mind. She'd cry in the car afterwards. Not here.

Noori looked up and saw the man run a hand through his hair, reigniting her urge to brush it. She tried to dismiss the odd fantasy, but the urge only grew.

Should she anonymously send him a comb in the post? Maybe he had so many other priorities that he couldn't get one for himself—maybe because it broke and there *was* a cost-of-living crisis currently. She couldn't blame him, and she was going to become rich soon. She might as well start her noblesse oblige now.

"All the avenues for support are summarised in here," the man said. "Would you like me to talk you through it?"

Noori shook her head almost too vigorously, the image of having to pay attention while he continued to speak making the decision for her.

"Thanks," she said and then put the booklet in her bag, convinced she was going to forget all about it but feeling committed enough to the prospect of reading it as soon as she got back into her car.

"I'll have a look. Thanks for your time."

~ ⌛ ~

Noori tried to rub the tiredness from her eyes for the umpteenth time that day but to no avail. She was at work, and she needed to at least look awake. Her almost perfect record of sleeping at a sensible time over the past couple of weeks had been ruined by the debilitating worry that had started to consume her before she slept and then again in the early hours of the morning.

She knew that once a habit was ruined, it was ruined. But there was hardly any time to dwell on that when she in fact had a very serious problem.

She was in denial about the time debt, and she was beginning to understand that the denial was really just her brain disconnecting from the matter because she just didn't know what to do, didn't know how to cope. She was a law-abiding citizen most of the time. She paid her taxes, served capitalism and had occasional moments where she was filled with nothing but existential dread. She was just like everyone else. An everyday person.

Surely, she couldn't go to jail because of a little time debt, right?

Wrong.

Noori's breakfast threatened to spill from her lips as she read another Reddit thread of someone in a similar situation to her. They had been put on a time ban for twenty years. A sacrifice she didn't want to make. Another person had chosen the option to just forward the time that they owed, losing the time with loved ones, and losing a loved one in the process. Some people did go to jail, but it was for a short period. They had also been fined and had a time ban.

She wanted to write up a post too, but she was paranoid about it being presented as evidence against her in the court of law and she knew all the advice other people were getting was exactly what she was going to receive, though probably with added judgement and conviction that she was an idiot.

She needed to be serious about the matter. She needed a plan and a plea to the jury. She hoped her life was a movie and that this was the low period before her happily ever after.

Noori huffed and pressed her cheek to the cool surface of the desk as she listened out for anyone who would walk past and thus motivate her to sit in an upright position and look like she was doing her job.

Outside of the crisis of her impending doom and her dreams of being on the big screen, Noori worked as a coordinator in a marketing firm, where she was able to share her creativity with the world through her outside-the-box but poorly thought-out ideas.

She loved it. It was a great balance of desk work and working with others in a field where she saw the result of her and her teammates' labour out in the world (though not always on the scale she exaggerated it to be).

She glanced at the to-do list she had written during their morning meeting. She had worked through it fast, ignoring her note to also read through the assistance booklet she had been given and then make a plan of action.

She bit her lip. They were going through a slow period at work, giving her time to do things outside her job, and despite that, she couldn't find it within herself to go in her bag and take her booklet out, even though she knew it had to be done.

Feeling a stab of shame, she added to her to-do list 'take booklet out of bag'. It was all about baby steps, after all.

She still couldn't get herself to do it and a ping from her emails saved her.

She had emails to respond to! And she loved responding to emails. It made her feel very professional and feeling like a *professional* professional made her work harder.

It was an ad from a food delivery company. Boring.

Who was she kidding? She was ahead of her work, thanks to her medication. If she worked too hard, her manager would only give her more to do, and Noori was only now starting to learn boundaries for herself.

"Everything okay there?" a voice called out, making Noori jump. She turned and faced Wallace, her manager. *Think of the devil.*

"All good. I sent the report through not too long ago," Noori said whilst laughing nervously. "Just taking a little breather."

"I just saw. You're so efficient. When you've got a minute, would you be able to assist the newbie with theirs?"

Noori nodded before she realised she had moved. *Damn it. The people pleaser strikes again.*

She liked her new colleague but at this moment in time, she really did not want to explain to them how she wrote up her reports. She didn't think about how she did them, only that they were done and management liked them. She couldn't explain her process because it was ingrained in her. While you remember how to ride a bike, you don't always remember the process.

Wallace left as Noori sat and pondered. She considered going to her colleague and bullshitting her way through some sort of an explanation, but she realised that, quite luckily, she was very busy right now, because she was going to take her booklet out of her bag and make a plan of action.

Noori opened a text app on her computer so she could write down her plan of action but then frowned and pulled out her notebook and her pencil case. She then took out the booklet and skimmed through it. She spotted one of the page titles which appeared to relate to returning time in increments.

She originally went to her friends for help and a plan, but why did she need to do that when she could just help herself?

First, she needed to assess where she could skip time before she did it willy-nilly and just make her life harder. She also knew she needed to stop borrowing time in order to understand how much she depended on using it. Feeling optimistic, she scribbled up her plan, first in her notebook, then on her laptop and then on the notes app on her phone.

After getting frustrated over the multiple ways of capturing her thoughts, she settled on her notebook. She drew out what her days looked like, thinking of a step-by-step plan to get herself together, and after thirty minutes, she smiled to herself.

This is it! Noori's five-step plan to freedom and success.

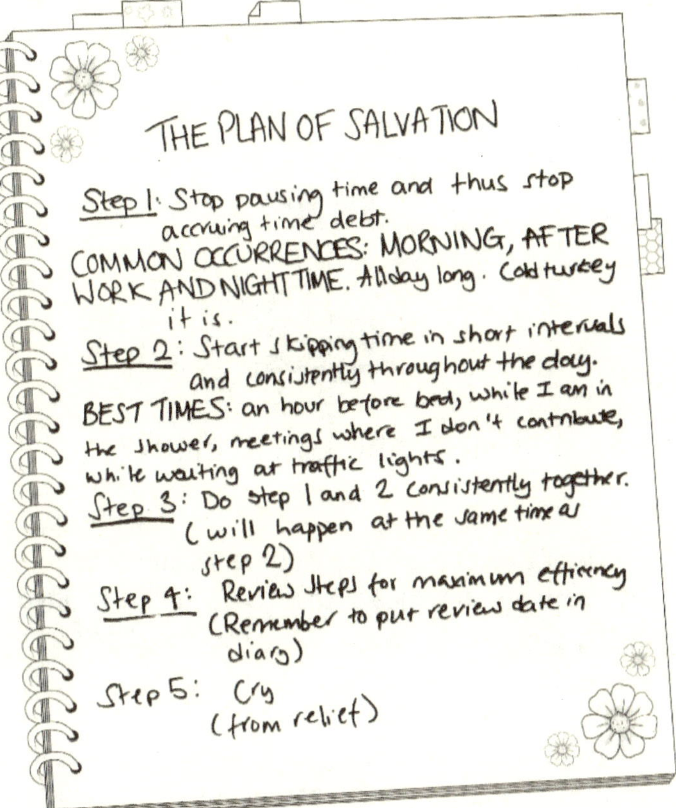

She reviewed the steps and her smile widened. It was perfect and if she played her cards right, she'd be free of her time debt by the end of the year.

3 MISS, ARE YOU ALRIGHT?

It was Day One of The Plan of Salvation and it was early when Noori realised how much she depended on pausing time. She'd had an idea, but she didn't know it was this bad.

Mornings were always something she struggled with, and she was always running late, getting up at the last possible second and then getting ready in a flurry. It made her efficient in the morning, but she had decided that it would be even more efficient to brush her teeth while she decided what to wear for the day while time was paused as well. That way she even got five minutes' more sleep.

Now she stood frozen in her room, looking at the time and knowing she was late but in denial enough to believe she could make it on time. She just needed to dry her hair, get dressed, do her face routine, make some breakfast, take her medication, get to work, park the car and get into the office. She was also sorely tempted to pause time to embroider a spaceship by the pocket of her new jeans. All within fifteen minutes.

Piece of cake, right?

No.

Noori texted her manager that she was running late at the time she usually rolled into the building, which was usually on the precipice of being late but on time enough that no one complained.

Once in decent shape, wearing a brightly coloured jumper to distract others from how dishevelled she felt and most likely undoubtedly looked, Noori drove to work panicked. She told herself that she had confessed her tardiness so she might as well take her time now, but urgency consumed her, making her rage at other late-goers on the road. Shouldn't they already be at work? Surely everyone wasn't as terrible as her, right? And if they weren't at work, what were they doing on the roads at this ungodly hour?

As she waited in traffic, Noori considered whether or not she was insane for giving herself only twenty minutes to get ready in the morning before she had to get going to work or she would be late.

She had to somehow figure out how to get herself up earlier. She reckoned she needed at least fifty minutes minimum to get ready in the morning if she wanted to do everything properly, whilst also accounting for forgetting things or getting distracted while her medication was kicking in.

It was hard. She couldn't do it. Mornings were the worst, truly the worst, and the embodiment of all evil and she didn't wish waking up from beautiful slumber and having to get ready for a whole day on anyone.

However, Noori did believe in a silver lining being found in every situation. She had always wanted to become a morning person. Actually, she kind of reviled sleep as a concept anyway. Why did she have to sleep when there were other things to do, people to meet and paydays to be had?

God, in a minute she was going to sound like she enjoyed capitalism.

When she got into the office, teary-eyed and guilt-ridden after Wallace gave her a warm welcome, she collapsed at her desk. She remembered that in the chaos it took for her to get in, she had forgotten to take her medication and she never carried it with her. *Today really is going to be a waste of a day.*

She felt like skipping the whole thing but didn't want to have to explain herself to HR again.

She was late enough that her colleagues had finished their morning meeting. Though, maybe that was a good thing because she usually paused time before she gave a report of her work endeavours to the team. She always felt that public speaking was awkward and weird, and she didn't get it as a concept, and she never knew where to look, and she low-key felt that the whole experience was so stressful she dissociated throughout and couldn't remember a thing about it afterwards. She always needed just a minute to pull herself together and practice to herself what she was going to say. Though despite this, it never went how she anticipated it would in her head but at least she knew what she was saying.

From tomorrow she was going to have to live without that minute of reprieve. But it was okay! She just had to get to work a minute earlier and have that minute on company time. She was already going to wake up earlier.

Another minute wasn't going to hurt her too much. She just hoped no one spoke to her during that minute.

Noori grumbled to herself, dissatisfied with the idea. Her colleagues were nice, and she liked it when they spoke to her. It assured her that they didn't wholly resent her behind her back.

She also experienced a lot of FOMO. She wanted to be included in every conversation ever and she especially needed to know about all the gossip happening around her. People often praised her in minding her own business but she didn't have the heart to tell them that she was so focussed on being the main character of her own life she forgot there were things happening outside of her story.

As she looked through her diary for the day, she realised that she had a lot of meetings to attend and that wasn't a good thing when she was unmedicated. She prayed no one made her write notes.

When she saw a meeting she knew would be nothing but boring to death and a waste of time, she groaned. But then she perked up. Maybe this would be a good opportunity to start skipping time!

She frowned. It was only day one of step one. She couldn't be skipping steps so easily. She had a plan, she had rules. She needed structure before she descended into chaos.

But she could be free of thirty minutes! No one spoke to her during this meeting, and she assumed most didn't know who she was, and she was never the note taker. As for having to know what the discussion was about and feeding back to her team? She was sure she could make it up. The meeting always felt incredibly unproductive anyway.

The consequences though! She considered herself an expert at skipping time during meetings. She would skip thirty seconds of every minute or skip every other minute but if in a rare circumstance she was called upon and she was sitting there unbreathing and uncommunicative, they would know, and she would be told off and she didn't want to be told off and for everyone to know what she had done.

As her present reality stood, Noori wasn't in a position to simply skip life thirty seconds at a time. She had a debt and had to be serious about it, and serious was what she would be.

~ ⌛ ~

Obviously, she was stupid, and it was a mistake. It wasn't news to her, but it was to people around her. Quite fortunately, she wasn't the only one who skipped time during the meeting, so she was hardly the villain. A team-wide reminder about time skipping during work hours had been sent out in response to her and her colleagues' actions. She was also given a talking-to by her manager, which inadvertently led to Noori unravelling about the matter on her hands. Though Wallace's face was warm with sympathy and concern, regret and shame flooded her and she declined the offer he gave for support on the matter. He had already supported her enough with the reasonable adjustments she had once requested.

Noori swore to herself to not skip any more time at work unless she was dawdling in the bathroom. She would have to repay outside of work, as well as finish off her project. With her heartbeat as her constant companion throughout the day, Noori knew the pressure of her debt was starting to consume her.

She was going to have to do it all. She had managed tighter deadlines when she was at university and at least now she was medicated. At least if she lessened her debt a bit by the hearing, despite her crime, maybe she could prove she was not worth the punishment. She had a life to live, and she didn't know how to cope with consequences.

After a couple of days of just getting through life with The Plan of Salvation, she slowly got the hang of it. Or at least that was what she told herself. It was difficult. She was late for things and felt quite disoriented when she was speeding up time whenever it was convenient (she started step two early), meaning she lost the context of what was happening around her.

She was just glad she was medicated. Otherwise, things would be a lot harder and she would pause time every time she got dysregulated or couldn't make a decision and just needed a minute or seventeen to pull herself back together. She suspected a lot of her debt had accrued when she was unmedicated, but she knew if she accessed her time records, she'd probably used the same amount of time unmedicated or not. She was forever falling behind on things and still hadn't done her laundry since the day she had been handed her fate.

She just liked to pause time! Was that a crime?

"How was the visit with the advisor?" Layla asked. They were on the phone and have been for an hour now talking about everything except what was important and pressing.

"Oh yeah," Noori said, recalling that such a thing had happened. "It was alright." She picked up a bag of tortilla chips off the supermarket shelf, considering it against its unbranded counterpart.

She couldn't really remember what had happened at the meeting. It was a week and already so long ago. She had lived a whole lifetime since.

"Did they...advise?"

Noori paused. She remembered the man's hair above everything else, but she could recall that he gave her something. Crap, where was it? "Yes, I got an information booklet."

"Have you gone through it?"

Noori cringed. "You know I can't read."

"Noori!"

"Layla!" she replied, though she shrank into herself when she remembered that there were people around her.

"Let's go through it now."

"I can't. I'm out shopping, remember?" She was getting snacks for the watch party which was taking place at the weekend. "Do you want me to starve you girls?"

"Of course not," Layla said, but then got back to the point. "But surely I can find a copy of it online and read it to you?"

Noori tensed and her mouth dried up. "I mean, I can't stop you, short of switching off the phone." She let out a nervous laugh.

She told herself that Layla was just trying to help.

"Don't worry. We'll be going through it together. I'm going to look for it now."

Noori left her friend to it and put the branded tortilla chips in her basket and grabbed some salsa before leaving the aisle. Before she remembered the next thing on her list, her gaze latched on a set of watercolour paints that were on offer.

She wanted it.

She felt herself reach out for it before she slapped her hand away, remembering the small scenic landscapes she had painted before she inevitably gave up on the hobby. She knew she had paints at home.

It wasn't the only infatuation she had picked up. She still had yarn from when she told herself she was going to knit all her friends a jumper. Riding boots from when she told herself she would become a professional horse rider. She remembered how much she had paused time to learn how to play the keyboard which was now a second table. She would never forget her stint with glassblowing. Embroidering on her clothes was something she still did every now and then. Drawing was the only thing that never let go of her, no matter what she did to escape it.

"Noori?"

"I am here, yes," Noori responded, startled. She quickly remembered why her friend had gone. Her heart thumped. She didn't want to think about her debt, much less talk about it. She had a plan, and she was figuring it all out herself. The week had been tough, but she was down a whole thirty minutes on her two-year debt.

She's got this.

Noori tried her best as her friend started going through it, starting with the contents page and 'an introduction to time debt' (which Noori had read three times before closing the booklet and hiding it from sight).

Fortunately for Noori, Layla didn't get very far either.

"My niece has just woken up. Give me a few to tend to her. You know, Aunty duty and all," Layla said. Noori heard cries in the background. "I'll call back in a bit, and we can go through more."

"Sure. Tell the little one she's still my best friend."

Layla laughed and disconnected the call.

She did not call back and Noori was glad for it because she didn't want to go through the booklet. She was reluctant and anxious and convinced that her life was going to end and so she did what she did best and imagined putting the thought into a box and then throwing that box out of a window. The anxiety from the situation was already making her shut down. She might as well do what was best for her current peace of mind. She had her five-step plan anyway.

Noori finished her shop and was on her way to her car, groceries in hand, when she saw people dressed in Universal Time Alliance uniforms. She very quickly recognised one of them as the one who had knocked on her door.

Not knowing what else to do, she ducked behind a car.

She knew it. They were onto her.

Of course, it wasn't going to be a simple matter of just attending a court case. She was a real time thief after all, and this must be one of their attempts at intimidation so she buckled under the pressure and accepted nothing but the maximum punishment for her crimes.

She remembered the movie *Matilda* and how the FBI sat outside the Wormwood residence spying on them. Was that going to happen to her? Were they listening in to her and getting more and more evidence that would lead her to a life sentence in jail? For nothing more than an insurmountable amount of debt and now, potentially something else too? She was unaware of what lesser crimes led to jail time. She knew that if the right person motivated her, she might be done for assault, but what was she committing without even realising? Fraud? Could you unknowingly commit fraud? She didn't know and was going to have to google it later.

She thought about her flat. It was a couple of storeys up. Would they rent in the building opposite and do a stakeout?

It was fine. She knew what she needed to do. If she got arrested, then she would simply say nothing at all until she spoke to her lawyer. Though, she didn't have a lawyer personally—should she? Wait, what if she got paired with one who didn't care about anything apart from getting their job done? Telling her to plead guilty for a lesser punishment? Could you change your lawyer if you didn't like them, and you were getting them for free? She pulled out her phone to look it up. It seemed like pretty important information to know sooner than later.

However, when she opened the browser on her phone, she remembered she hadn't finished googling what she had searched for before (can you get perfume refills) and it was something she still wanted to know. She opened a new tab, promising herself she would look at the other thing later before she jerked up and remembered that she was still hiding.

She should probably leave and go home. Barricade herself in her flat, take annual leave and then skip time until the watch party.

But did it matter? She had too much time to give. So much so, she was two years older than she actually was. Maybe she should bite the bullet and say hello to everyone in 2026?

God no, she couldn't do that. She was just about to make her big break. She was going to be a famous animator akin to Walt Disney. She was going to have her own studio whose name she hadn't yet thought of and, as a result, was losing sleep over.

Not only that, but she had so many things she wanted to do, and she didn't want to miss the lives of people around her. She was going to have to find another way. Looked like she was still going to be held in a chokehold by her five-step plan.

"Miss, are you alright?"

Crap. She was still crouching down. She looked up at the concerned onlooker, trying to get herself up at the same time but she floundered backwards at the sight of them.

It was one of the Time Alliance agent people things. They were coming now to get her. This was it. Was she going to relinquish herself freely? Or go down with a fight?

"I'm alright," she said, pushing herself up unsteadily and not taking the hand of the Time Alliance person. She was glad to find that it wasn't the one who knocked on her door, but she was worried that they would use it as an opportunity to cuff her. "Just needed a break. You know what they say, if you don't take a break, your body takes one for you." Noori laughed nervously. "Anyway, thank you kindly for your concern. I really appreciate it. I need to get going though. I hope you have a good rest of your day, kind stranger."

Maybe if she sucked up to them enough, they would pity her and let her go. They would not seize her, especially as she had been trying so hard to reduce her debt. She was making their jobs easier.

"No worries. Take it easy."

Noori nodded and then dashed to her car, almost hitting her shopping bags on every available obstacle on the way.

When she got in and locked the doors, she looked back to where the Time Alliance people were and saw they were walking with their colleague into a fast-food place, probably getting lunch. She buried her face in her hands and took deep breaths. It was getting to her and she didn't know what she could do or if there even was anything she could do until the hearing.

~ ⌛ ~

Noori went through the animation again, her eyes trained on the slowed frames. Her friends were coming over in a bit for the watch party and while it was more or less done, she was getting it to perfection.

She wasn't pausing time anymore to help get a seamless finish, so she was going to lose sleep over it. But it didn't matter. She needed to perfect it and she needed time for that. As her court date was the same day as the deadline, she'd have to be early.

She had a week left until both, and two weeks after that it would be the showcase. In the grand scheme of things, it was no time at all, so she definitely didn't have the time to be arrested.

After perfecting it and the showcase, she would be able to work better at reducing her debt. She tried her best in the moments she could, adhering to step three religiously at the expense of her sleep and eating. It wasn't wise and she could feel the impact of it, especially as she knew that her medication wasn't working as best as it could, but it was all she could do. She would just have to apologize to her doctor later.

Hopefully, the courts would see how good she was and give her a chance to rectify her ways. At that point, she would commence step four. She would live very frugally with time. Noori looked on the bright side of the matter. She would become very efficient and quick at everything and with the little cost of not being able to watch TV, hang out with her friends or participate in any other fun thing.

But she would have her showcase and a reduced debt. She would have it all, and she would only be amazing because of it. She couldn't wait to talk about her life in interviews in due time. The time debt would be nothing more than a minor setback from the distant past.

Noori would have it all.

Noori lost herself so much as she went through the frames that she almost had a heart attack when her alarm rang. Something she had set earlier and now alerted her that she needed to get ready for her friends.

She snoozed her alarm, promising herself one last five minutes before she stopped. She knew she was nitpicking, and she knew she should leave the animation as it was but knowing herself, she knew that she would just go over it again and again until the night before the showcase.

When her alarm buzzed again, she got up and started changing the set-up of her room. She placed all her fluffy blankets on the ground, along with mismatched pillows. Then she cleared all the pieces of paper she had on the wall and set up the projector she had borrowed from Layla. Next, she took out snacks and drinks and set them on a small table. She was also going to order a pizza when her friends arrived.

Noori smiled to herself as she put on her fairy lights. Now all she had to do was dim the lights when the short movie started. The movie which her friends were seeing for the first time in its entirety after only ever teasing them with snippets. She knew her friends would be positive with the feedback, but she wanted to wow them. To show how amazing her animation and she was.

A sudden stab of paranoia jolted Noori and she briefly considered whether she should cancel. But before the thought could fully form in her mind, there was a knock at the door.

That was her friends, unless it was another person from the Universal Time Alliance. She shuddered but then pushed the thought away. It wouldn't be them because she was already due in court next week. It was going to be fine.

She got the door and found Kiran there. The friend who was always on time. She remembered then that Emaya would be late even though she was the first one to text they were on their way.

"We're staying the night, by the way," Kiran said by way of greeting as she came in, a carry-on slung on her shoulders.

Noori scoffed. "I'm not sharing my bed with you."

Kiran put down her bag and took off her shoes. "You'd prefer one of the others and be attacked?" Kiran asked and moved to the couch.

"Um, actually, I'd rather be by myself," Noori said, closing the door.

Kiran shrugged. "You're taking one of us. Two on the bed, two on the couch."

Noori sighed and sat by her friend. Somehow her place was the favourite for sleepovers. She just hoped that they would end up sharing horror stories. She loved the thrill of it, even though it meant she couldn't sleep afterwards. "I'll think about it. Now, tell me how it's going."

"Good. Same old with work though, but I'm more curious about you," Kiran said. "Your time debt. Are you prepared for the hearing?"

Noori shuffled on her seat. "I have a plan to reduce my time debt."

Kiran tilted her head to the side. "Why do you have a plan? Don't you have to just prepare for the hearing?"

To prove herself was the truth, but Noori wasn't going to say that aloud. She knew she should speak to a legal representative, but she wasn't going to meet them until the day of the hearing, a few hours prior.

Noori shrugged. "I just want to do everything I can to stop anything from getting any worse, which starts with a plan to stop the overuse of time." She paused and then added, "I think."

Kiran pressed her lips together as she considered what Noori said. Noori hoped it was enough to not get any more questions.

In the group, Kiran was her longest friend. Her first supporter and her ride-or-die. Emaya and Layla were similar in a sense, but it was Kiran who'd adopted Noori when she was on the cusp of doing something stupid in her first year of university.

Kiran was the one Noori felt most comfortable breaking down in front of, in the few times that she did, and it was vice versa too. She felt bad for not telling her the truth. She was deserving of it and wouldn't judge her fears in the slightest, but Noori couldn't do it. Her body seized up at the thought of disclosing how she felt about the matter.

Her friends would just think she was an overreactive idiot anyway. She was Noori and always had a good thing going. She was scared of sharing all her silly little nightmares of being in jail for life without parole. She knew that she was blowing the situation out of proportion, but she just needed to get on with it by herself. She's got this and she didn't need to burden anyone else.

"You know you could talk to me, right?" Kiran said, surprising Noori for a moment and making her think she could read her mind, but she realised that Kiran was just being polite.

"I know and I am always grateful for it."

"You don't need to be grateful, and you don't need to wait for me to offer."

Noori nodded. "I know."

"Good," Kiran said and then fished out her phone from her pocket. "Where are those silly girls? They promised they would be on time."

"If Emaya is picking up Layla, they're both going to be late," Noori answered.

Noori saw Kiran text, a smile creeping up on her face and only getting wider.

"Why are you smiling?"

"Am I not allowed to smile?"

"Unfair," Noori complained, dissatisfied with her counter.

Kiran laughed. "I'm just excited. You've been talking about this forever."

Noori's heart fluttered. "I have, haven't I?" She mused. "I hope it lives up to your expectations."

"From what I've already seen, it has."

Noori's smile widened, her heart warmed from the praise. She switched the conversation again to Kiran and her endeavours until Emaya and Layla came. They too with their overnight bags. She was almost offended they didn't tell her about it.

After causing a ruckus about what pizza they should order, they moved to Noori's room where she had set up.

"This is so cute!" Layla said and immediately settled herself down on the pillows. "It feels so real."

"Well, it is real," Kiran said and then turned to Emaya with a pointed look.

Noori furrowed her eyebrows as she watched Emaya process the nonverbal hint Kiran was giving. After a moment Emaya beamed. "And we have something to make it more special!"

"What are you talking about?" Noori asked, looking at Kiran then Layla and back again as Emaya left the room. They both shrugged and Noori rolled her eyes.

She shifted from foot to foot as curiosity ate at her, but she told herself to be patient.

"Now," Emaya said outside her room. "Close your eyes and hold out your hands."

Noori looked at Layla and Kiran again, her eyes narrowed, but they betrayed nothing.

She followed Emaya's request. "I hope you know that this is a big show of faith towards you."

"We would never betray you, Noori," Emaya said, amusement in her voice.

Bracing herself and rocking on her heels, Noori waited for Emaya. After a moment something soft, like a piece of clothing, was in her hands.

She opened her eyes and saw that she was right. It was dark blue, a shade that was almost too familiar to her. She unfolded it and upon realising what it was, tears came to her eyes.

"Girls!" she cried, holding up the T-shirt that had the title of her animation on it. The blue was the same shade she had used in her title background. "What is this?"

She lowered it and saw that her friends had similar T-shirts.

"Well, we have to take this watch party seriously, don't we? We're your first fans after all," Kiran said, as if it was obvious.

"We have to do this properly," Layla affirmed. "It was Kiran's idea and Emaya sorted it all out. All I had to do was get the logo and the colour, which you already sent to me."

Tears fell from Noori's eyes. "I can't believe it. This is so amazing. I love you girls so much."

"Don't cry and ruin it," Emaya said and then lowered her voice, "I think the colour might run."

Noori laughed and wiped her eyes. "You're the best. All of you. Thank you so much."

"I know," Kiran said and started pulling the T-shirt on. "Now, let's get watching. You've made us wait forever."

Noori nodded and with them all matching, she started the film.

~ ⧗ ~

Hours after the viewing, Noori and her friends were still awake, talking about *Errant's Law* and how they were all excited to be on the red carpet, which they were all sure would be sometime soon. They spoke about their love lives or their lack of. They spoke about all their dreams, nightmares and wishes for the future, all on the floor of Noori's bedroom with snack stains on their matching T-shirts.

They giggled as sleep started to overcome them and as Noori's eyelids drooped she thought to herself that this was perfect, and she didn't want anything to change. Sure, she hadn't achieved anything yet but tonight had been even better than her daydreams of watching *Errant's Law* on the big screen.

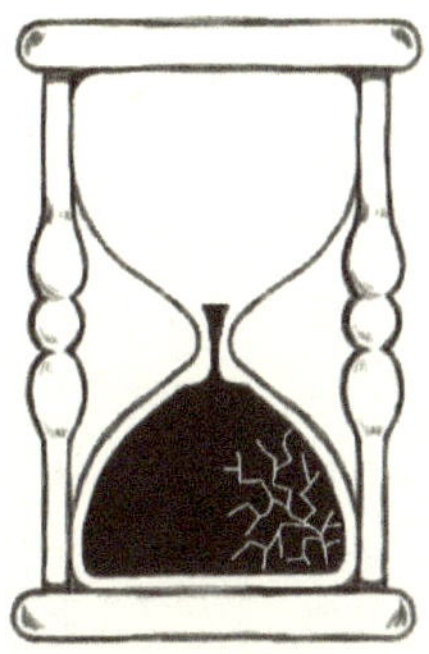

4 I HAVE ADHD, YOU SEE

It was twelve hours before the deadline when Noori cursed out into the night. She knew she should've just submitted it. At least then she would have regret not panic. Regret was a spice of life, and you could potentially argue that panic was one too, but Noori was sick of that flavour.

She sat in front of her computer, her hands shaking and her eyes wide. The word 'shit' fell from her lips continuously like a mantra. She'd just noticed that she had been inconsistent with the colours of some of the backgrounds when it changed from scene to scene. She couldn't believe how she'd managed to miss something so obvious and now that she couldn't unsee it, it distracted her from the story.

It was midnight now, and the deadline was at midday. She had been so confident in her finishing of the animation with tonight being when she submitted that she'd procrastinated her final check to minutes ago. Really, she should've submitted it the morning after the watch party under the supervision of her friends and just not thought about it again, but her perfectionist tendencies demanded that she pore over it until the last possible moment.

She grumbled as she thought about the watch party. Her friends hadn't commented on the colour change, so was it truly a big deal?

Well, whether it was or not, it bothered her immensely and she didn't know what she was going to do.

She needed to consider her options. It was now midnight, meaning that she only had ten hours to correct all the mistakes, get enough sleep and get to the meeting with her legal representative before her court hearing which she hadn't prepared for aside from imagining herself as Elle Woods.

Noori gnawed at her lip, her mind racing. What should she do? *What should I do?*

She wasn't that attached to her sleep, so she didn't mind missing it for the night (lie. She really, really wanted nothing more than to take some herbal tablets, wrap herself in her blankets and drift into sweet oblivion). She also didn't feel comfortable submitting something with such a rookie mistake. She wanted perfection for the silly little story she had slaved away a lot of her early adulthood doing. She wanted to have her moment and prove to herself and those around her that she was amazing and all her yapping about her project wasn't for nothing.

She would have to pause time.

It would be fine. She only needed a bit of time to sort it out. Nothing major that would rack up her debt and alert the concerned authorities. She needed an hour max.

~ ⏳ ~

It was longer than an hour. Much longer. Six hours later, she called it quits and nodded off to sleep. When she woke up, she realised it was still the previous night.

Shit. She had forgotten to resume time and had slept for a grand total of—Noori did a double take—she had sixteen hours on her pause timer, meaning that she had slept for a long time. There was no way the Time Alliance was going to ignore that especially with the court hearing so soon. She had no way of rectifying it.

Maybe she should just stay like this forever. They couldn't catch her if she was in a small pocket of stopped time.

Her breath quickened. Why was this happening? She just wanted to submit her damn masterpiece and be famous. Was it too much for a girl to want?

Now she was definitely going to be imprisoned.

But she was also making things worse by not unpausing time, wasn't she? She had heard horror stories of nefarious plots being foiled by the Universal Time Alliance when people paused time for illegal purposes. They probably had a way around it somehow. They were probably on their way to her now.

She slapped her cheeks, giving her body a shock to compose herself. She needed to get it together.

She was going to submit her animation and skip forward enough time so she could make it to her meeting with the representative and then at the court hearing, she would plead her case on her knees to the jury. As long as she could get her work submitted, everything else would work out.

Taking a breath, she started time again. The unnatural stillness from her surroundings disappeared and she faced her laptop, the brightness of the sun that filtered through the window now making her squint and look at the time.

Noori rubbed her eyes and looked at the time again.

Huh?

What?

It was just after four p.m. on the Friday of her deadline and court hearing.

"Wait," she said quietly, her mind churning. "Wait, wait, wait, wait, wait!" She got up from her bed and started pacing the length of the room. She looked out of the window, and it was in the middle of the day alright. She had a great view and could see dozens of people going about their day. She marched back to her laptop and checked the time again, then on her wall clock (which was wrong anyway because she kept forgetting to change the batteries) and then her phone.

"I started time! I didn't skip it! I—" she cried out. She looked at her wrist. Her debt was still as it was before without the sixteen hours she had accrued.

She had missed her deadline and court hearing.

She had missed her deadline and court hearing!

SHE HAD MISSED HER DEADLINE AND COURT HEARING!!!!!!!!!!!!!!!!!!!!!!!!!!!

What was she going to do?

What was she going to do??????!!!!!!!

She froze as if she were in a catatonic state, her chest rising and falling rapidly as the situation dawned on her.

As much as she wanted to mope about losing the chance to submit her life's work, it hardly mattered. She had missed her court hearing where she was going to plead her case and now she would face sanctions and she had no idea what that was going to look like.

~ ⌛ ~

After an hour of muttering incoherently to herself and staring into space, Noori was finally able to get her body to move. She made a ready meal and ate it while it was still hot and took her medication, knowing it was the wrong time to take it, but she needed to be able to think straight and with less noise in her head.

It was a glitch. Something that happened rarely and more often when time was paused for long. It would naturally forward to what time would be if it hadn't been paused at all and now, she was here.

She knew she had to contact the Time Alliance, if they already weren't heading this way with handcuffs ready for the kill. She had to explain that she hadn't meant to miss the hearing and it was an accident. She had no intention of missing it at all and that there was a glitch, and it wasn't her fault.

Oh, who was she kidding? It was her fault. She had paused time, hadn't she, and then been stupid enough to fall asleep without resuming it again. Most people didn't pause time for that long because of the incidence of a glitch being higher and while Noori preferred to live life on the edge and did often have time pause for considerable lengths, a glitch had never happened before.

Tears came to her eyes. Who cared about the colours of the background when no one was seeing the animation after all? The event was also a super rare once-in-a-lifetime (yearly) submission as well. This was going to be her year. She was going to manage her time debt and have it all.

And now? She had neither. She had nothing. She was going to be prosecuted and jailed and everyone was going to be so mean about it because she accidentally missed her court proceedings.

Noori facepalmed, wanting to die. It was all pretty dumb. The whole thing. The back story, the motivation and the execution. Now she would suffer the consequences of her actions with no light at the end of the tunnel. This was the end.

She found the number to contact the Time Alliance and started the call. God, what was she going to say to them? There was a glitch? She knew a lie when she saw one and she knew they wouldn't believe her. What was she even doing accruing more debt anyway?

She placed the call on speaker and saw she had a barrage of messages on her phone, from the *Neurospice girls* group chat, a colleague who wished her luck on her deadline and her manager who wished her luck for the court hearing. The legal representative had tried to contact her as well, and Noori wondered briefly if she should grovel to them but decided against it.

Kiran, Layla and Emaya had messaged her separately too, all of them having the same flavour in messaging—all wanting to know how things were going with both the deadline and court proceedings and concerned she hadn't said anything all day.

She couldn't tell them.

They would just have to live with the fact that she would never contact them again and while the chapters of their friendship were fun and full of light, all things came to an end. The quartet would become a trio. It would be like if the Bratz broke up or something.

It would be sad but they would all have to live with the decision she had made. It was fine. Who needed friends anyway?

She sat on the verge of tears as she imagined her life without her friends. She had moved to the city away from her family. She spoke to them often and went over sometimes, but her friends were the family she'd picked up along the way.

"Hello? Hello? Anyone there?" a voice called from the phone. Noori jerked to attention, too busy moping to remember that she was calling someone.

"Yes, yes, I'm here," she replied. She pressed the phone to her ear.

"Hi there, my name is Jo. How can I help?"

Noori sniffed. "Well, you see, there was a glitch and, and, and it meant, I didn't know—I had fallen asleep! I didn't mean it and I had every intention of attending and sorting it all out and I'm so so sorry!"

Shit, shit, shit! Tears fell from Noori's eyes, her throat started to ache and her voice croaked. She needed to stop crying! This was so embarrassing. They would probably think that she was doing this on purpose to get sympathy points and as a result they were going to hate her more and she was going to spend more time in jail.

"Oh my god, how embarrassing—please, I need a minute," Noori said and lowered the phone from her ear. This was so stupid, all so very stupid. She tried to deepen her breaths, trying not to ruminate on what the person on the phone was thinking—that she was pathetic on top of being a criminal.

Noori tried to remind herself that crying was a normal bodily reaction, and she wouldn't judge someone else for it, so it should be okay, right?

The thought was hardly a consolation. She attempted to slow her rapid breaths before she placed the phone back to her ear. She didn't feel better at all.

"Hello?" she croaked out, tears still falling from her eyes.

"Hi there, are you okay?"

"No, I'm not," Noori said. She wiped her face, but more tears fell. "You see, it all started a couple of weeks ago. I have a massive time debt and I didn't see the letters. I didn't even know there were letters and okay it's my fault I should've looked and kept an eye on how much time I was taking but it was a lot and I didn't have it in me to be better about it. I have ADHD, you see, and while it's not an excuse, it's a reason and it was difficult, and everything is so difficult and that is why I pause time so much because I just want to feel like I am doing as well as the people around me. Life is hard, and I just want a chance, you know? And I get so much joy from the praise and the compliments. It makes me want to do so well but I can't do it all the time and if I can't do it all the time, people are going to find out—they're going to find out that I'm not good enough and I'm not ready for that. My life will end."

Embarrassment burned through Noori. What was she actually saying?! She wanted to stop but didn't know if she could.

"More importantly, I have this dream. I want to be an animator and make fun little movies and be on the red carpet and just have a good time, you know? When I finally got medicated, I was finally able to do it, get myself together enough to finish what I had once started. There was a deadline today for an opportunity I have always been working towards. But I realised last night there was a mistake and I needed to fix it and listen, I have been so good with my time debt. I had a whole five-step plan to help reduce it and it was slowly working but last night, I needed time. I needed time, okay? And it was at the cost of a glitch. I worked until I slept, forgetting I had paused time and when I woke up, I realised, and I resumed it because that's what you do. I was even going to forward time for the most part too. I was going to submit my project and then attend the hearing but there was a glitch and now it's hours later and I missed the deadline and I missed the court hearing and I'm in so much trouble now, aren't I? Just tell me quick."

After she stopped speaking, her throat felt scratchy but that was nothing on the flush she felt all over. What was she doing? She held her face with her free hand. God, she was so embarrassed. What was she doing trauma dumping to a random stranger on the phone? Embarrassing, embarrassing!

Maybe she should just switch off the phone now and call again and hope it wouldn't be the same person.

But it would be so much worse if it was the same person! Noori sighed to herself, keeping the call on. She didn't want to risk it.

She waited for Jo to speak, feeling glad that she wasn't in their situation but guilty that she had put them in it.

"I understand. It sounds like you missed your court hearing today because of a glitch? Can I get your name and details so I can access your record?"

Noori nodded, forgetting that the person couldn't see her. She gave her details and waited for them to continue.

"Ah, so you had a hearing at midday today to discuss your time debt of two years..."

Noori sniffled again. Jo was starting to sound judgy but she needed to be strong. You had to be tough if you were going to be stupid.

"It's a serious offence and missing the court case because of borrowed time doesn't help your case either, Miss. You mentioned you have ADHD?"

Noori nodded again but after a moment vocalised affirmation.

"Have you spoken to your specialist about this?"

"No. My doctor says valid things sometimes and I'm not ready to hear the voice of reason," Noori said and then caught herself. She really was running her mouth. "Isn't she just going to say that I reaped what I sowed? I am of sound mind, you know; I doubt I could get any leeway for just being an idiot."

"Well," the person said, sounding almost as if they were going to agree with her, "they might be able to write a supporting statement for your condition. There is a booklet given when you are flagged up for a court hearing. Did you read through it?"

Noori felt like crying again. It always led back to the damn booklet. The bane of her whole existence.

"I'll be honest with you. I have it. I've tried reading it but it's just really difficult and it's so stupid. I know it's just a booklet but in the war of Noori and the booklet, the booklet conquers me every time," Noori confessed. She bit her lip and awaited Jo's judgement.

"Okay, that's fine. I can arrange for you to meet with someone to go over your options with you in person or over the phone if that would be helpful?"

"I think so," Noori said. Shame and inferiority welled up inside her, making her nauseous. She should just be able to read the stupid booklet!

"I'll also put on the record the reasoning for you missing your court hearing and you'll hear soon about what happens next."

"Is someone going to come to where I live again?" she asked, a chill creeping over her.

"Not if you respond to the letters first."

Noori huffed to herself. "Would you be able to send an email? I'm better with emails."

"I'll note that on the record."

"So do I just need to wait now to go over the booklet with someone?" she clarified.

"Yes, but we would recommend you speak to your specialist about this too. They might be able to help."

Noori remembered lying to Dr Vallant's face when she first asked about time usage. She hoped that she would forgive her. "Okay. I'll do that."

"Great. Now, Miss, take it easy. It's going to be fine, okay?"

"Thank you," Noori said. "You've been very helpful and nice. Thank you and sorry for all my nonsense."

"It's fine. Is there anything else you need assistance with today?"

Noori shook her head. "No, thanks. Have a good evening. Love you, bye."

Noori terminated the call as soon as she realised what she said and she slapped her forehead, feeling like she needed to be under constant supervision. She flopped on her bed, her body a bit lighter. She was grateful that at least she had confessed the truth. Now, she just had to face the consequences.

5 NO ONE HAS IT ALL

Noori delighted in the feel of cool sun on her face, making her smile to herself. The blue sky that stretched on for miles raised her spirits, and she wanted to skip along the street. It was early and the High Street wasn't busy yet. Shops had started to open their shutters and she promised herself she was going to have a solo date after she had completed her mission for the day.

Right now, she was the main character. It mattered not what her final destination was, only that she was here in this moment.

A moment that did not last long enough.

"Noori!"

Noori ran. She knew that voice and she couldn't get caught by them. Not in life and not in death either. Besides, because she ditched her car and decided to take the scenic route, she was probably on the precipice of running late anyway.

It was Kiran, easily the most formidable of her friends. She needed to escape. Now.

"Noori!" her friend called out again, her voice loud and breathless. She was running too. "Why are you running?"

Noori didn't pause to answer. The question was a trap, she knew it.

She had ignored her friends quite selfishly since she missed the court hearing and the deadline. All their phone calls, texts and when they knocked on her door. She knew they knew she was there, but she hoped they got the undelivered message that their time was up.

Noori knew she was being ridiculous but she was just so embarrassed.

Panting already, she stopped as soon as she rounded a corner and out of sight of her friend. Hopefully, Kiran would be just like her, and Noori would now be out of mind.

After taking a moment to catch her breath and straighten her clothes, she walked slowly in the direction of her doctor's clinic, whom she had an appointment to see.

She was fixing all her life's problems. She was going to face her future, starting with pleading her case to Dr Vallant. She wasn't far now, and she had already rehearsed in her head all the grovelling she was going to do.

"There you are."

Noori yelped and thrashed as someone grabbed her wrist, tugging her in their direction. She opened her mouth to start a ruckus but was promptly stopped.

"Don't scream, you idiot."

Recognising the voice, Noori turned to her friend. "Kiran?"

"Oh, so you don't have memory loss?"

Shit, Noori thought. Kiran was smartly dressed in black and glowering at her. *Shit. I thought she forgot all about me.*

Noori's mind was racing. What should she do? Cause a scene and accuse her friend of something so their friendship was irrevocably ruined? So much so it ruined her friendship with Emaya and Layla too?

What would she even say? She wasn't good at making up stuff like this on the spot. Her mind was empty.

Crap, I'm taking too long to respond.

Not knowing what else to do, Noori just smiled and said nothing.

Kiran's eyes narrowed at her. "Explain yourself."

"Sorry?"

Kiran's hand tightened on her arm. "Why have you been ignoring us?"

Noori tilted her head to the side. "I literally have no idea what you're talking about." This was good. The dumber she acted, the better.

"Liar. You pretended you weren't at home two days ago. Didn't you?"

"What are you talking about?"

Kiran's nostrils flared, telling Noori that she was furious, and she shuddered at the sight of it. She had never been the object of her friend's rage. Maybe playing dumb was the wrong thing to do.

What was she doing anyway? *God, this was so dumb.* She was so dumb.

Before she could say anything, an alarm from her phone buzzed. She was going to run late for her appointment, and it wasn't something she could miss and neither did she want to be late for it.

"I have an appointment now. I can't miss it."

Kiran gave her a hard look and didn't let go of her. Noori started twisting her arm, testing her friend's strength.

"I promise I have an appointment."

"Promise you'll explain yourself and then I'll let you go."

Noori ground her teeth. "Not fair."

"You're the one who isn't fair. You can't just ignore us, you know," Kiran said but then her voice broke. Noori looked away. "Everything was great at the watch party. What happened?"

Testing her friend's strength more, Noori turned away as she said quietly, "It's better this way."

"What?" her friend said, exasperated. "Don't be stupid. You don't get to decide that."

"Well, I am stupid, aren't I?" Noori retorted. In a strong, swift pull, she yanked her arm away and started to run towards the building where she had her appointment, trying to scrub away the memory of the pained look on Kiran's face as she did.

~ ⧗ ~

Dr Vallant paused before addressing Noori, who stood nervously at the door to her clinic room, red-eyed and breathing rapidly.

"Come on in and take a seat," she said.

Noori silently moved to the seat in front of the bespectacled older woman, who observed her before she spoke. "How are things?"

Noori looked down at her fingers which were clasped together on her lap. "Things could be better." She sniffled. "How are you?"

"Good, thank you," Dr Vallant responded. "Did something happen?"

"I'm experiencing a breakup. Not with a romance but with my friends," she said and sniffled again. Noori told herself to get it together. She wasn't going to cry in front of her doctor again. "Don't worry. It's not the reason why I asked for the appointment."

"What's been going on?"

Bracing herself, Noori explained the matter. From the beginning to her sitting in the clinic now. She couldn't stop thinking about Kiran and the crumpled expression she was wearing when Noori left her. She really was the worst.

"You should've mentioned you were struggling with borrowing time. It's not uncommon for people with ADHD to accumulate time debts," Dr Vallant explained after Noori concluded her monologue. "It's actually one of the conditions that has the highest risk of developing a time debt."

Noori blinked, feeling quite stunned at the revelation. She had been ready to start apologizing to her doctor for her lie and for getting into this situation. "Really?"

"That's right."

"Then why did the man, the advisor man, not say that?" Noori asked, referring to the first advisor that she had seen. Thinking back, he'd been really unhelpful. "I showed him my diagnosis letter and everything."

"I'm not sure how much the advisors know about ADHD specifically. We had a conversation about time usage during our first appointment, didn't we?"

Noori nodded and then bit her lip. She had adamantly told Dr Vallant that she never had an issue with borrowing time but in reality, she was ashamed of her usage. She hadn't considered something like this would happen where the truth came out anyway and she would be even more ashamed of herself.

She was also scared that even though her doctor had diagnosed her and prescribed her meds, she was going to turn around and say she didn't have ADHD after all. The odds were probably extremely low but no one really spoke about the imposter syndrome that persisted post-diagnosis.

"I'm sorry I lied. I hope you're not mad," Noori said, wringing her wrists and wondering what she should do if Dr Vallant was, in fact, mad at her. Was this going to be another break up? Should she leave before things got worse?

"I'm not mad at you," she said. "I can understand why you felt you couldn't talk about it. I was also new to you."

Noori blinked. "Really?"

"Yes really."

Noori let out a sigh of relief and wondered if she should confess to all her other much less significant lies. She opened her mouth but then changed her mind. She would send an email. Dr Vallant should hopefully forgive her by the time of their next review.

"Have you thought about what's driving your time usage?" Dr Vallant asked.

Noori frowned, knowing what she was getting at. "I thought you were a psychiatrist, not a psychologist."

Dr Vallant smiled. "Even so, there are many reasons people choose to borrow time. I know that people with ADHD might use time to help compensate for some of the things they struggle with, but in doing so, it makes them lose a handle on how much time they have used. Even when they are on medication."

"Can you blame me though?" Noori said. "I'm just... I'm..." She looked away towards the window. "I'm trying my best but it's never enough. I get a chance when I use time, and things have gotten better ever since I started taking medication. I'm finally starting to feel like a functioning person." She fidgeted with her fingers, ignoring the discomfort in the base of her stomach as the truth spilt from her lips. "With time, I can have it all." Tears came to her eyes, but she blinked them away.

"Noori," Dr Vallant said. "No one has it all, so it's not fair of you to expect that from yourself."

It was true.

She looked at her lap, not wanting to look at her doctor. In her wild chase for perfection, she had failed and ended up worse than where she began. She knew it was a fool's dream, but having done almost everything in a manner that was wrong or dysfunctional, she'd finally had a chance to do things in a way that didn't garner judgement.

It was refreshing and she was addicted to it.

"I'm told," Noori answered, shuffling in her seat. Her gaze moved everywhere around the room except to where her doctor was sitting. She didn't want to talk about this anymore. She had this conversation often with her friends. She didn't want it here. "Thanks for the reminder. I know it's something I have to work on." Noori moved to the edge of her seat. "Can we talk about the time debt? The person on the phone said that talking to you would be helpful."

Dr Vallant paused for a moment before she nodded. "Of course."

~ ⌛ ~

Noori looked down at The Plan of Salvation that she had written up and frowned.

Now that she had spoken to multiple professionals about her time debt, she realised it really was a stupid plan and she had learnt that it didn't matter that she was going to show herself as serious to the court. The facts were that she had accrued a ridiculous amount of debt and any moral or righteous character she had wasn't going to save her.

Going through the booklet should have been the first thing she did. After she had an appointment to go over the whole thing, she realised that it was very helpful in explaining the process and where she could get support from. Noori learnt that maybe she needed to put aside her pride and think about the easier option rather than the Noori option. If it was something that helped her, she should take it, especially as she did have her struggles. It was why the support was there in the first place. She just hoped that she learnt from this.

She had the option to consider a self-imposed time freeze and coaching around managing life without borrowing time, something that was very easily accessible to her thanks to her diagnosis of ADHD. With the supporting letter her doctor had written, she was able to opt for the option and it freed her. At first, she felt like she had lost a limb but she knew that it was the right choice. Now that she had no control over time, she just had to accept things how they were.

Her doctor also spoke to her about adjusting her medication, something Noori hadn't really thought about during the chaos. Her catastrophic thinking and restlessness had made the past few weeks difficult, and with the change Dr Vallant had made, she felt so much clearer in her mind.

Now she just had a meeting to attend with some of the senior advisors instead of having a new court proceeding and she would be offered easier and more structured ways to repay the debt which didn't involve crying. The Time Alliance was also able to adjust the ratio of time taken vs time to give back, meaning that instead of giving back two years, it would feel more like one and a half years. Noori didn't understand the math and knew that the time left to give was still a lot, but it felt easier than before.

Altogether it was going to be smooth sailing from here. There was nothing more she could do.

Noori moved to rip the page out of her notebook but then decided against it. Instead she neatly crossed out each step, wanting to use the page as a reminder that she didn't have to do things alone and that maybe that wasn't so much of a bad thing.

~ ⌛ ~

Noori was home on her own when she watched the live stream of the event she had planned on submitting her animation to. The showcase was an in-person event where creators would be able to show off their projects, giving them exposure and press and the opportunity for some investment by renowned animators and directors who attended.

She would've been there had she submitted. It would've given her great exposure and she would've had her dreams come true. She was so proud of the work she did, and the feedback she often got from others was glowing. She knew not everything was for everyone, but she really believed in the story she told.

But she wasn't there. She was at home watching the event through a private livestream which was expensive, wrapped in blankets, in the T-shirt her friends had made and in the dark. She wanted nothing more than to sink into the earth and disappear. She'd missed this opportunity and for what? Some mis-coloured backgrounds? *Embarrassing*. She should've just submitted it anyway and then told anyone who noticed to mind their own business.

She watched as people were interviewed on the livestream, telling the audience about their inspirations and journey to where they had gotten, making Noori feel bitter. She had already practised the answers in the shower and now she wouldn't be able to use them. What a waste.

She had even tried contacting the organisers afterwards trying to explain her situation, but they didn't allow her submission.

Feeling increasingly frustrated the more she watched and deciding she didn't need this kind of negativity in her life, Noori reached over and closed her laptop screen. At the same time there was a knock on her front door. It was a knock which very quickly became knock*ing* and it was increasing in intensity.

She bristled. Was she under attack? Was she about to get robbed? Was it the Time Alliance?

No, no, no, it couldn't be them. She pushed away her paranoia. She had sorted things out with them. It was just a matter of time of giving back what she owed.

Now, she spent her time thinking about her project and how stupid it was that she had missed the chance for submission. She knew things happened as they did but she had really been looking forward to this opportunity. Crushed dreams always left their own bruise even if there were more opportunities ahead.

"Noori! We know you're in there. Open up now or I'm breaking down the door," Kiran called out.

Shit, it was worse than the Time Alliance. It was her friends.

She hadn't spoken to Kiran since the last time she saw her, and guilt seized her because of it. If anything, abandoning her friend with no explanation should've sealed the deal on the demise of their friendship rather than her idiotic actions.

She also wondered what led to them ambushing her now. It had been weeks since Noori had first decided to be dumb. Did Kiran rally the troops and were they now at war?

Noori got up and moved towards the door, which was vibrating from all the ruckus they were making.

"Don't just stand there. Think about my poor hands! You're going to have to give me a massage in a minute," Layla grumbled.

"Yeah, right after we punch you in the face," Emaya called out.

Noori cowered backwards. Three punches in the face? That felt like a bit much, no?

"No, you deserve much worse. You don't deserve us at all," Kiran stated. She sounded the most annoyed and it just made Noori more nervous.

"Then why are you here?" Noori asked, her voice loud. She startled and covered her mouth. Why did she speak? Now they definitely knew she was home.

Though who was she kidding? Her car was parked outside and she hardly went anywhere this late.

"Noori!" they all called out in unison, the volume of it jostling her but not as much as the emotion in their voices did. They missed her and she missed them, and she really was an idiot.

An idiot who didn't want to let her friends go.

Quietly, she closed the distance between herself and the door, her hand on the latch.

"No punches," she said.

"No promises," they replied.

Noori opened the door anyway, smiling to herself and was greeted by her friends throwing themselves at her. They hugged her so tightly she wondered briefly if she would've preferred being punched instead.

"Idiot!" they all yelled at once, making Noori laugh.

"I know, I know."

They pulled away from her, giving Noori space to breathe but space to breathe was also space to cry and before she knew it, tears dripped from her eyes. "Sorry, girls. I'm sorry."

"Idiot. Cry like that and I'll end up crying too," Kiran said, her eyes welling up. "Idiot."

Noori almost laughed but a cry broke out of her instead. She stumbled but her friends caught her before she fell.

They took her to her bed, putting away her laptop and scolding her for not putting on the lights as they made themselves at home.

Layla held her, Kiran ordered some food and Emaya started setting up the room as Noori settled down. Once she did, she found the floor had a throw on it with pillows, pizza and drinks, making her smile but making her stomach churn. She really was stupid, and she knew it for certain when she saw they were all wearing their *Errant's Law* T-shirts, probably having gone to the showcase to find her.

"You want to know what's going on, don't you?" she said to them, knowing that even if they didn't ask, she was going to explain herself anyway. She wouldn't be able to face them otherwise.

"Well, the main reason we're here is because we went to the showcase to ambush you, but you weren't there. We asked one of the organisers and they said that no one of your name ever submitted and that's when we knew something was wrong," Emaya explained and passed Noori a slice of pizza.

"Only something serious would've gotten in the way of that submission and we didn't care if you pushed us away as a result of it. We needed to know and so we came straight here," Layla further explained and took a slice off Emaya.

"We also tried to look through arrest logs—what? Even though I saw you, we don't know what the result of your court proceeding was," Kiran said.

Noori rolled her eyes. It was true. They knew nothing of what she had been up to recently. It was predominantly either working, moping or returning time.

"Listen. We won't force you to tell us anything but try that again and I'm stealing your work. That shit's amazing," Emaya said, now handing Kiran pizza.

Noori let out a little laugh and took a bite of her pizza. She looked down and saw they ordered her favourite.

"It's all stupid anyway. It's nothing too serious but pure ridiculousness on my part and I'm ashamed of all of it," Noori confessed, placing the pizza slice back in the box.

"Even so," Kiran said, smiling softly, encouraging Noori. "We'd love to hear it."

Taking a deep breath, Noori recounted everything her friends knew about the debt and how things had developed until the glitch and then everything after that, including how the situation, in a way, had solved itself even though she was so stressed about it for so long. She really didn't need to take everything on herself.

She looked away as she spoke, never focusing on the girls for more than a few seconds to save herself from seeing their expressions change into anything akin to rejection or judgement and consequently make her feel worse.

There was silence afterwards, everyone getting on with eating as they took everything in. Noori's impatience mounted as she ate. She needed to know what they thought, whether they were sick of her or not, whether they hated her. She considered it was a long shot, but anything was possible.

"Okay, but I don't understand the part where you decided to ignore us? Or did I miss something?" Layla asked.

"You didn't miss something. I—it's, well," she mumbled. Her face heated up because not even she remembered the reason anymore. "I was so ashamed of myself because of messing up. I thought you guys would look down on me because of it. Because you know, I have things 'together' and I just couldn't face you guys when I didn't have it all. The whole situation is stupid and so un-Noori like that I didn't want to tell you guys and the only way to do that was—"

"To never speak to us ever again?" Emaya finished. "And that way, the 'image' we have of you won't be tarnished because we'd never know?"

Noori nodded. It sounded so ridiculous now that the truth was out.

All three looked at her in varying shades of disbelief. Noori tensed and her stomach flipped. Had she misjudged the whole situation? Were they going to reject her after all?

"What, are you a robot or a person? And before you answer saying robot, no. You are wrong," Kiran said. "You are human. Of course you're going to fuck up."

"And we definitely do not think that you have it completely together or that you have it all. Girl, you are amazing, but you are literally a calm serene swan who is paddling like mad under the water. We know you work hard," Emaya said.

Noori blinked at her.

"Noori, you are deeply unhappy with yourself, and I would like to know why," Layla said. She grabbed Noori's hand and squeezed it. "Do you really think we're friends with you because we think you're amazing? Sure, it's a perk but I would say my favourite thing about you is that you're the same flavour of idiot as me. You and me? We literally are the same person and fine, you're kind of valid with your whole avoidance thing because I might have done the same thing but then I met you and I know that you always get me no matter what I do."

Noori was frozen. It was like her guts had spilt out and everyone agreed that it was red and gory and completely normal. While it felt absolutely invasive, it felt nice?

"I can't help it, can I?" Noori moaned, her voice heavy, and she was sure that she sounded pathetic. Was she going to laugh or cry? "I am just like this. I am this."

"What you are is too hard on yourself. Honestly, girl, you could do less than the bare minimum and we'll love you still," Kiran asserted, shifting on her cushion so she could move closer to Noori.

Noori looked down, taking in what she was saying. Her doctor was right. Maybe she should've let Dr Vallant psychoanalyse her. Next time she'd have to say she was sorry, and she had free rein over all the mind-reading that appeared to come with being a psychologically informed professional. Maybe it would be helpful. Maybe she should go find a therapist herself.

She looked up at her friends then away. She felt raw, vulnerable and frankly quite disgusting. A part of her wanted to ask her friends to leave and another part wanted to dissolve into a puddle. There was also a small part of her that felt like weeping because how healing was it to hear the words she was being told?

She knew she was hard on herself. She had heard so a thousand times, but she didn't know how to be anything less. She liked working to a high standard and doing a good job but so much of it tied into how she felt as a person. Having ADHD and operating in a world that was not made for her was hard enough already. The medication helped but it wasn't everything. How could she be any less hard on herself when everything was hard?

All she wanted was to be good, to have pride in herself and to be loved.

As she pondered, Emaya continued to speak. "Noori, we now know what happened around the submission and the court hearing. It's kind of funny in a miserable way but we don't regard you any less because of it."

"If anything, it would be nice if maybe you didn't think of us as so unloving of you, and this isn't a criticism," Kiran said. "Your love for others and more specifically us is up to your own high standard, is it not? Why don't you hold us to the same?"

Noori nodded. She let out a choked breath which she tried to hide but they all heard it and brought her closer to them, her tears now falling freely on them.

"We don't expect you to change anything tonight about the way you regard yourself so don't use what we are saying as an excuse to set yourself another standard," Layla said against her hair.

"And we do not believe that you 'have it all'. That you have all the good and none of the bad," Emaya explained. "No one could have only the good, you know. And like you literally are the worst person to share a bed with, so you're far from perfect anyway."

They all let out their own variation of a laugh and Noori made a note to herself to offer to share her bed with Emaya tonight.

After they pulled away, all of them with tears in their eyes, Layla spoke. "We're really sorry about your project. We know that you worked hard on it."

Kiran and Emaya nodded.

"It was amazing and we loved every minute of it," Emaya assured, rubbing Noori's arm. "I am still in awe that you were able to create such a thing."

A moment passed, their breathing the only thing Noori could hear aside from the ticking of the broken clock. Kiran reached out to hold her hand. "We're gutted for you, Noori. Let us grieve this with you as well."

Noori nodded and reached over to hold on to her friends again, fresh tears falling from her eyes. There was warmth inside her, growing and blossoming. She hadn't submitted her project, and she still had a time debt, but she had this, so in her own way, she did have it all.

PRE-STORY BONUS CHAPTER: NOORI SUBMITS TO THE EXPO

Noori wondered who she should thank first, the universe, the newsletter, or herself as she read through the competition section of one of the many animation-related newsletters she had subscribed to. They had all played a part. The universe placed the email at the top of her inbox and the newsletter existed with the golden opportunity, but Noori actually opened the email, which was the critical thing. So, she thanked herself.

She knew she was at work and should look like she was, well, *working* but she took out her notebook and started to scribble the details. The competition was hosted by the National Animation Expo, which called budding animators to submit a minute of their animation, whether it was part of a movie or series. The clip had to be unpublished and the deadline was in three months.

"I could totally pull something together in three months," she told herself. She had heard of the competition before but her series, *Errant's Law*, hadn't been in a presentable state and she hadn't had the mental and emotional capacity to even think about submitting. She knew that this was not the case now. Feeling relatively settled on her ADHD medication over the past few months, she had been working hard on her baby. Now, she had completed most of the storyboards for a significant amount of *Errant's Law* and had even finished animating some scenes.

Noori perked up when she realised that she could probably even submit something right now, because she absolutely had a minute animated! She had finished the beginning of the tale, which would be the best thing to submit. For pulling in an audience, Noori couldn't think of anything better!

Before she made a note to submit the beginning as soon as she got home, she paused. She read through the submission rules again and frowned when her gaze fell on the stipulation that each entrant was limited to one submission.

Whatever she submitted would have to be good. *Really good.* The best thing she had ever created. Maybe she should think over what scene would be the best to submit. She pressed her lips together as she thought about some of her favourite action scenes and the parts which resonated with her soul. It wouldn't be good to limit herself so early.

What if none of it is good?

She bit her lip as knots formed in her stomach.

Can I really do this?

Noori shook her head and sent the ready-and-waiting spiral of doom away. "Winning doesn't matter," she told herself. *I just have to submit something. Submitting something bad is better than submitting nothing at all.* All she had to do was try and she had three whole months to find the perfect scene and polish it up.

Noori underlined the deadline date she had scrawled in her notebook multiple times before she decided to put a weekly reminder on her phone. "I'm not going to wait until the last minute," she told herself, knowing what she was like.

I'm not going to do what I did with last month's presentation or what I've done with basically everyone's birthday present this year. She promised herself that she wasn't going to spend 98% of the time before an event or deadline simply pondering about what she was going to do.

It was fun. She enjoyed musing about the actions she could take and what would happen as a result of the different choices she made. It was kind of like playing a choose-your-own-story. She felt like she was solving a puzzle to find out what would be the best way to go about something – the most optimal and efficient way. However, thinking took her nowhere.

This time was going to be different.

Noori then set herself an alarm so when she got home, she would look at what she had animated already. From there on she would decide what scene she would focus on. She was not going to obsess over the detail and she was not going to let it consume her life for three months. Noori was going to get it done.

~ ⌛ ~

Anyone who knew what Noori was like – herself included – would know that her saying that she was going to do something reasonably and sensibly was her lying. She promised herself that she didn't mean to lie but she couldn't help it that having a coherent, stepped process was a sure-fire way for her to rebel.

Three months had passed and Noori stared at her tablet, the blank screen staring back at her ominously. It was the day of submission and here she was doing exactly what she had sworn to herself that she would *not* do.

She wanted to swear to herself that she would never do this again. But let's be real, when it came to staring a deadline straight in the eye, crumbling under its unforgiving gaze and still making it, this was not Noori's first rodeo, nor would it be the last. One truth she knew wholeheartedly about herself was that not only did she work well under pressure – she *only* worked under pressure.

Now she sat, the pit in her stomach deep and her throat feeling tight.

"You're getting distracted again," Kiran sang as she tapped Noori's shoulder. Noori blinked up at her friend.

Right – she had invited her friends over to help her stay focused. They were participating in what they liked to call 'let's get it together, together' time where they all had a task that they needed to complete and they would hold each other accountable.

Kiran was finishing a painting that she should've already given to her cousin. Emaya was emailing her ADHD team to not discharge her and apologising that she had not asked for medication for four months, amidst other life admin, and Layla was finishing some work she told her manager she had already submitted.

"Do you think I'm insane for doing this?" Noori asked, the question directed to no one.

"Yes," came the chorused response.

Emaya looked up from her laptop and said, "But we love you anyway," and blew Noori a kiss.

Noori huffed a laugh, thinking that she hadn't really told her friends half of what had happened since she had learnt about the competition. On the evening of finding out about it, instead of following her plan of action, she decided to google other animation competitions. She read about the life stories of various judges, looked at the accomplishments of previous winners and how their lives changed after having their big break, with one of them actually managing to get one of their stories on the big screen, and she read all the hints and tips everyone gave.

Basically, nothing had gone to plan.

Noori decided to shift her focus to start thinking tactically, with her first course of action being to research the animation industry. It was a business after all and she did work in marketing. She wasn't about to let her hard-earned expertise go to waste. She knew bits and pieces about the field but she knew that she was overdue for a full education, so what better time was there than now?

She started her studies, which primarily comprised googling a lot, watching some YouTube and TikTok videos, reading Reddit posts and listening to a couple of episodes of a podcast. She even bought a book about animation which she was certain was still sitting in the bag she bought it in and she took her friends to a local film exhibit.

Noori learnt a lot, overwhelmingly so. After dreaming about her main character, Alissa Errant, lecturing her about frame rates, Noori decided she deserved a break. This ultimately started the series of events that brought her to this moment. Her overwhelm lasted a week where she couldn't think about animation without wanting to trauma dump. Following this, Kiran invited her and the girls for Paint and Chai at her place. As she always did after spending time with her friends, Noori felt revitalised. However, before she could use her newfound will to animate, her period came and she decided that she was the tiredest person who had ever lived. She wrote off the week and suddenly she was here.

Noori shifted her gaze to the upper right-hand corner of the screen, and she watched in horror as the clock struck 10 p.m. Her nostrils flared and panic paralysed her brain. It was almost funny how fast those three months had flown by. *Almost.* She had two hours left to submit until the portal closed, or Noori would lose her chance at fame.

It's fine. I can do this!

Fortunately, the past few weeks hadn't been a complete waste. She spent the time deciding – thinking – about which part of her animation she should send off. She wanted to give her story justice. Alissa was like her, in that she had to operate in a world that was not made for her. The story was an adventure about how she defied odds to achieve her dreams, got the treasure *and* led to the establishment of *Errant's Law*.

"I mean, are you sure what you had before doesn't work?" Layla asked.

Noori froze. In that moment, she realised that her friends were blissfully unaware that she, in true Noori-style, had changed her mind about what she was going to submit *again*. She wasn't about to tell them of course – for both her sanity, and theirs.

It's fine. The submission only asked for a minute of animation. She could totally have a minute finished.

Plus, she had already told everyone she knew (she even emailed her doctor), so she was left with no choice – she *had* to make that deadline.

Kiran watched Noori carefully over her easel. "Are you going to be okay?" she asked. "It'll be okay if you don't submit, you know?"

Would Noori be okay after doing the ADHD version of the Walk of Shame? Probably if she moved country, changed names and started a completely different life.

She took a deep breath. "I'm going to go to my room to pause time for a little bit." She looked at Kiran pointedly and said, "I'll be fine."

"Do you want chai? I was just going to ask Kiran to make some," Emaya said, turning to Kiran with a hopeful look in her eyes.

Noori shook her head but huffed a laugh when she saw Kiran roll her eyes, put her equipment down and head towards Noori's kitchen. Noori picked up her tablet and notebook, moved to her bedroom and shut the door behind her. She settled in her desk chair, connected her tablet to her computer and considered her options. To no surprise to herself, Noori had done a complete 360 and had decided that yes, she would submit the first minute of the beginning. There was no better hook, after all.

She started by seeing what she had to work with. She opened the file and sighed in relief when she realised she had more than enough content and it was in decent form. "Psht, this'll be a breeze," Noori said to herself, finding that she felt up for the challenge. She might not even need to pause time at all!

Before she watched the animation, Noori decided to log into the portal to reread the submission rules for the final time. It would be a shame if she missed anything after all.

She read it lazily, her gaze and mind drifting as she took in the instructions and she almost missed something that she hadn't realised she had missed the first time.

Her heart thudded.

With as much composure as she could scrounge up, she got up from her chair and threw herself on her bed, her hands covering her face as she began to fake sob into her pillows. "Why am I like this?" She wailed, her voice muffled by a plushie she almost risked bankruptcy to win.

After about a minute of lamenting in her covers, Noori rolled over and looked up at her ceiling. However, before going down another spiral, she got up to sit back at her desk. With her face in her hands, she reread the submission rules and started to consider her course of action.

It turned out, Noori could submit a clip that was longer than a minute. The maximum was ten minutes. She had just stopped reading when she saw that the minimum was a minute.

She knew she could just continue submitting a minute and feign ignorance, but it would be such a waste!

What was she going to do?

What was she going to do!

She groaned. She knew she didn't know how to read properly! She always misread things and then selectively remembered the information she was sure was correct!

Noori started to whimper into her hands. Should she just quit? Should she just lie? It was highly unlikely for her to be chosen anyway! No one was going to know if she didn't do it.

But...she already paid the fee and she could've eaten with that money!

Noori lowered her head to the table and started banging.

She just wanted to do a good job on her submission! The National Animation Expo was the place where her interest in animation had first been conceived after all!

Why does life hate me? Why does having ADHD suck so bad?

"Girl, you okay in there?" Kiran called out. She sounded close, as if she was just behind the door.

Noori jolted upright. *Crap,* she temporarily forgot her friends were here. "I'm fine! Just thinking!"

"Well don't think too hard. It sounds painful," Emaya called out, her voice also sounding close.

Noori rolled her eyes and pushed away the shame of her meltdown being caught by her friends. "I'm fine," she called back. She straightened her posture and slapped her cheeks.

"It's fine," she whispered to herself. "I'm just being dramatic. I literally have the first ten minutes done."

Noori went back to the rules to read the keywords – *up to* ten minutes it said. She told herself that she didn't have to submit ten minutes, just maybe more than a single minute. She played the beginning and found that as she watched it there was a nice sweet spot to stop at around four minutes in. Noori looked at the time and hissed.

She then shrugged because she *had* time.

She cracked her knuckles, watched the clip again and noticed that the animation was not smooth throughout and some of the colours could do with some work as well, but that was fine.

Noori then paused time.

~ ⌛ ~

Without incident and obsessing only a little bit over detail, Noori, after three hours, was done. Satisfied, she unpaused time and saw that she still had over an hour to get the clip submitted. She felt a wobble of unease in her belly, and while she knew it was not a good habit to have, pausing time was key for her staying on top of things. She touched her wrist, where a band covered where it was recorded how much time she owed. It was best she didn't check. After all, if it had become a problem, she would have already been informed by the Universal Time Alliance.

Smiling to herself, Noori got up and left her room to share the good news with her friends.

"Back so soon?" Emaya asked blowing over the hot cup of tea she held in her hands. It reminded Noori that while it had been three hours for her, it had only been about ten minutes for her friends since she was last with them.

"Have you submitted?" Layla asked eagerly.

"No, I wanted to ask if you all wanted to watch beforehand?"

"I thought you would never ask!" Kiran said, swiftly putting her paintbrush and palette down. She ushered everybody towards Noori's room, where they all crowded around Noori's desk. Her heart thrumming, Noori pressed *play*. As the clip played, she switched between watching the screen and her friends' reactions. She smiled when they laughed at the same bit that had tickled her for months, and her cheeks started to hurt when she saw that they were all equally captivated.

When the screen darkened, Noori laughed at how her friends turned to her, their expressions displaying a tangible urge for more. "Well?" Noori asked.

"It's amazing!" Emaya complimented. "I can't believe you've made this with your own hands!"

"I can't believe I'm friends with someone who's a whole animator," Kiran said. "You are incredible!"

"Is that it?" Layla asked, her eyes still on the dark screen. She turned to Noori. "I want more."

Noori beamed. This was exactly what she wanted.

Noori then felt Kiran's gaze on her. "I thought you said you were animating the standoff?"

Noori felt another wobble in her stomach. "I was but I took your advice and I used what I had," she said and then shrugged, her gaze on everything except her friend. "I think it would be better to give that part of the story the time it deserves, instead of rushing it."

Kiran smiled, satisfied with her answer, and Noori felt like she could breathe again.

"Well, we know you wanted something good and this was amazing," Layla said. "But before we start celebrating, you should submit."

Layla was right. A part of Noori felt so accomplished she wasn't feeling too bothered about the competition.

"Okay, stay with me while I do it," Noori asked her friends.

Noori moved to sit in her desk chair, her friends still crowded around her. She went onto the website, logged into the portal – glad that she had already filled in all her details – and she attached the video. A thought of her submitting the wrong thing and all her hard work going to waste then played in her mind, making her shudder.

"What's wrong?" Emaya asked.

Noori answered blankly, "Nothing. I just imagined I submitted the wrong thing and the judges might be watching a blooper I needlessly animated of the characters having a rap battle."

The girls started snorting with laughter as Kiran remarked, "I really want to watch that."

"I wouldn't be surprised if they watched that and you won," Layla chimed in.

Emaya agreed. "Yeah, if I were the judge, I'd fast-track you to the finals."

Noori turned and glowered at her friends. "Now is not the time for you to be changing my mind. Please, I am begging you."

They laughed again, and Kiran turned Noori's head back towards the screen. Unfortunately for Noori, she had so many copies of her animations, and they all had unhelpful names. When she located the video, she renamed it THIS IS THE FINAL FINAL VERSION OF THE ANIMATION FOR NATIONAL ANIMATION EXPO COMPETITION 2024 and attached it to her submission. She took a deep breath and pressed *submit*.

Together, the girls watched the loading screen and then a message popped up onscreen, saying that the submission was successful. Noori cried out, "It's done! I'm free again." She felt weeks of pressure melt away from her, making her want to jump up and do things now that she was free, but she also felt a wave of fatigue. She pushed the latter to the side. "There's so much space in my head." What hadn't she done in that time that she had been absorbed in this? What had she neglected?

"When did you start this, again?" Layla asked.

"A week ago," Noori answered, knowing that they were referring to the standoff idea which she had started from scratch.

Emaya hissed through her teeth. "You should probably sleep first."

Noori briefly wondered whether she should wash her face or shower first, but shook her head and beamed widely at her friends. "No, we celebrate! Because I am one step closer to having it all!"

AUTHOR'S NOTE

I wrote this story during a two-month unplanned medication break in late December 2023 and early January 2024. The idea came to me when I was at the gym with a friend. On the cycling machine, I was reflecting about how there isn't enough time and how cool it would be if you could just pause time to get things done. I then started thinking about being able to pause time if you had ADHD and how you would probably forget to un-pause time because 1) you were too distracted and 2) you forgot you paused time in the first place. And then I started thinking about how such a person would get in a lot of trouble from the 'time' police and lo and behold Noori came to be (sort of; I spoke to two friends about it who encouraged me to try writing it and begrudgingly I started thinking of a plot).

Truthfully, I was never interested in seriously writing a story where the main character has ADHD. However, I decided to take advantage of my chaotic unmedicated ADHD state and I challenged myself to complete the story by the time my one-year anniversary of diagnosis came around, which was at the end of January 2024.

The story kept changing as I wrote it and it didn't end how I anticipated (I think there was supposed to be a part where Noori was meant to be arrested?). I've tried my best to let the ADHD ADHD, and honestly, I've never had so much fun writing something. Noori's internal world came to me so naturally that there have been parts of the writing hardly untouched by editing because it came out so authentically the first time.

After writing it I decided that it would be worth sharing. I had first started trying to find an agent but it became apparent to me that trying to get something published is a luck game and it is hard to publish a novella. I went to a writers' conference in May or June and after some encouragement from a friend, I decided to self-publish.

While short, Noori's story is close to my heart. I can't say that this story is a self-insert, but I can't deny that it isn't, either. Noori's struggle to 'have it all' is something I have struggled with as well and I know that this is only fuelled by living with ADHD, especially after receiving the diagnosis. Last year, when I received the diagnosis and the medication, what else could I possibly need? I *can* do it all. I can do *everything*. Nothing can hold me back. As you can imagine, it has been quite the journey.

The most surreal part of this journey is when I reread the story months after sending it to agents and I found that I just didn't resonate with Noori like I did when I wrote it. In the months since, on my own journey of understanding ADHD and myself, I found that I no longer wanted to 'have it all' and I am more than happy to ask for help and thank goodness for that.

I am not sure how others would receive this story, but I hope you have enjoyed Noori's chaos and maybe even resonated with her a little bit whether you have ADHD or not.

ACKNOWLEDGEMENTS

There are many people I wish to acknowledge, firstly to thank them for directly supporting me in the making of this story and secondly, those who have supported me in my journey of understanding and living with ADHD. This story would not have existed without you all.

I'm not sure who exactly to start with first without offending anyone but where's a better place to start from than the beginning?

Aliya, I'm sure you saw this a mile coming. You've probably been expecting this even, because who else do I thank before you? This story is a fruit from a seed you planted when we were thirteen. I never thought that making up a story together would lead to this thirteen years later. Thank you for being my beginning.

Sid, my absolute guardian angel. As we have previously discussed, I have no need for an acknowledgements section if you are not in it. You, who entertains every story-related thought that comes into my head. My creative partner in crime. I have been blessed by your presence in my life and in my journey of writing. Thank you for every minute.

Leesa, for all the talking we do about our creative pursuits, I did not think that there would have been one where we would be working together, even though just a little bit. Thank you for all the conversations and rants we have about the creative process; thank you for always being a listening ear and for all your advice and support. Most of all, thank you for making Noori come alive before my very eyes and thank you for the cover, which I simply adore to pieces.

Anam and Maariyah, my neurospicy beta readers. Thank you for your time and excitement in being among the first readers of this book back when I was self-conscious that I had somehow messed the whole neurospicy experience up.

Thank you to Rebecca for being my copy-editor and proofreader. I was nervous about sending out my work to you but you have been easy to work with.

And now to those who have supported me on my journey!

Asha, I am always so sorry for and so thankful to you for every time you allow me to yap about the ADHD demon that's possessed my brain. From helping me get to my assessment to my one year of diagnosis anniversary cake and beyond, you've been on my journey as much as I have and I am eternally grateful.

My (baby) sister, as you know you are very important in every writing endeavour (and not only because you once proclaimed so). Thank you for being so excited for me and being the one who listens at home. Thank you always for your support.

I also thank my work girlies, neurospicy and otherwise, who have been part of my journey. You are the friends I made along the way and your friendship, patience and acceptance have helped shape me into who I am today and have helped make this story possible. You know who you are and please don't be mad I didn't name drop you. I have been confused around the laws of name dropping in an acknowledgements section and I'm not the type to explicitly ask (that ruins the surprise!). On this limb, I also want to thank my colleagues, supervisors and other friends who are probably sick to death of how ADHD is my everything. Thank you for always listening and supporting me.

My (ex?) psychiatrist. You knew it was going to be a journey before I did and I'm not sure how much nonsense I've subjected you to because of it; thankfully the ADHD means that I've forgotten. *Noori Has It All* couldn't have happened if you hadn't picked up my case and become my doctor! Thank you for all your support.

My therapist, even though I was paying you; thank you for doing such a fantastic job at helping me heal and make sense of myself. I am out of my Noori-era and into another and you have been the biggest conduit in this process—thank you!

Lastly, I would like to acknowledge myself because I actually did not think I would get this far. I can now say that I am a published author. I better not let this get to my head...

www.ingramcontent.com/pod-product-compliance
Lightning Source LLC
LaVergne TN
LVHW051013080826
845145LV00009B/2603

* 9 7 8 1 0 6 8 5 2 2 4 1 3 *